"What are you doing now? Green palm fronds won't burn."

Dathan lifted one dark eyebrow at Adrella, but continued retrieving more fronds. "I'm going to build us a shelter for tonight. We ~~can~~ tinue to sleep in the tower. It's t~~oo~~ ~~dangerous~~."

Adrella was du~~bious~~ mosquitoes?"

Dathan grinne~~d~~

"How gallant o~~f~~ ~~you~~ sarcastically.

Dathan's grin turned into a full-throated laugh. Adrella's heartbeat quickened, her eyes going wide. Never had she heard Dathan laugh. Truth be told, she had rarely even seen him smile. His dark features were lightened by his humor, and Adrella noticed for the first time just how devastatingly attractive Dathan could be.

"Don't worry, Adrella." He chuckled. "I won't let you be carried off by mosquitoes, nor any other thing that resides on this island."

Adrella swallowed hard, realizing just how attracted to Dathan she had become. Did he include himself in that statement?

DARLENE MINDRUP

is a full-time homemaker and homeschool teacher. Darlene lives in Arizona with her husband and two children. She believes romance is for everyone, not just the young and beautiful. She has a passion for historical research, which is obvious in her detailed historical novels about places time seems to have forgotten.

DARLENE MINDRUP

There's Always Tomorrow

HEARTSONG
PRESENTS

Recycling programs
for this product may
not exist in your area.

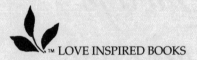

™ LOVE INSPIRED BOOKS

ISBN-13: 978-0-373-48652-6

THERE'S ALWAYS TOMORROW

www.LoveInspiredBooks.com

Printed in U.S.A.

For his anger lasts only a moment, but his favor lasts a lifetime; weeping may remain for a night, but rejoicing comes in the morning.

—*Psalms* 30:5

For Remko—thank you for marrying my daughter
and giving me the three greatest treasures
I could ever have: Jaime, Matthew and Ryan

And for Joniessa—thank you for marrying my son
and helping him to finally feel complete

Chapter 1

Cape St. George Island, Gulf of Mexico, 1868

The skiff's bow lifted high on the crest of the whitecapped waves of the Gulf of Mexico before plunging down to the trough below. The fine, misting spray settled lightly against Adrella Murphy's face. Smiling, she threw her head back to allow her long red curls to blow freely in the warm late-October breeze.

Her father glanced at the darkening horizon worriedly. "I should'na ha' allowed you to come with me on this trip, lass," he told her. "There's more than a mere storm a brewin'."

Adrella smiled at him, her voice soothing. "Oh, Da, you worry too much! We've handled some pretty rough weather in our time."

Snorting, her father tightened his hold on the tiller. Peering out at her from underneath the brim of his battered cap, he told her regretfully, "Aye, and your mother, God rest her soul, would have me hide if she knew the way I was a raisin' ya. 'Tis no life for a lady."

Adrella reached across and squeezed her father's hand reassuringly. They had been through this argument numerous times already. There was nowhere on earth she would rather be than right by her father's side. He had been mother *and* father to her for the past fifteen years. She could barely remember her mother, having been only five when she died.

A school of dolphins crested near their boat, their lively chatter bringing a smile to Adrella's face. She watched as they quickly dove and disappeared from sight.

"They sense the approaching storm," her father told her, his anxious gaze once again studying the far horizon.

She studied her father's weathered face and could visualize what she would look like in another twenty years. The ruggedness etched with time on his features did nothing toward diminishing Mangus Murphy's good looks. His fiery red hair was salted with grey, but his green eyes still glowed with healthy vitality. But whereas her father was a handsome man, his strong features passed on to his female offspring were less than flattering.

Adrella wrinkled her freckled nose at the idea. Her own green eyes flashed at the thought of the insult she had just received that morning. Jasper Howard had offered his hand in marriage, not because he loved her, but because he wanted someone to help raise his children.

"After all," he had stated rather categorically, "it's not like you're likely to receive any other offers."

Her Irish temper had surfaced quicker than a breaching whale. When Mr. Howard had left her presence, his ears had been red from the lambasting he had received. Still, her own tears hadn't been far from the surface. Didn't she already know that she was a plain woman? She had heard it often enough in her time. Yet her father adamantly claimed that God would send her the man He had destined for her, and she would know what true love could be. Just like Da and Mama.

Her lips curled up at the thought, her eyes gentling. Oh, to be loved like that! Even after all these years Da's green eyes still glowed when he talked about his Mary. Adrella could barely remember how her mother looked, the memories growing dim after all this time, but she still remembered the shared laughter. The love.

She turned her smile on her father. "You know I have to learn to fend for myself. If something happens to you, who's going to take care of me?"

Instead of the snappy response she had expected, her father's frown deepened. "I've been thinkin' about that."

Surprised, Adrella could only stare. What was her father thinking? And why should he be concerned about her now? Thoughts racing through her head for some explanation, her mind focused on the fact that Da had been to see Dr. Taylor only two days ago.

Her face paled considerably leaving her whiter than the sand on the beach, her freckles even more pronounced. "What are you saying? Did Dr. Taylor say something about your health?"

Something serious flashed through his eyes momentarily, but then he gave her one of his heartiest laughs. "Now, Adrella, me darlin'. Don't go giving me to the Great Banshee just yet!"

Frowning, Adrella was unconvinced. She knew her father almost as well as she knew herself, and he was hiding something. That hearty laugh had held just the merest hint of panic in it. As often happened in times of stress, her Irish brogue came out thicker than usual. "Faith, and 'tis not something to joke about!"

Her father's face grew serious. "No, Adrella. 'Tis not." Reaching across the space between them, he cupped her chin in his calloused palm, stroking her trembling bottom lip with his thumb. "But when the time comes, love, I want to know you'll be taken care of. I know the good Lord is lookin' out for you as well as your old da can, but it would sure set me mind at rest if I knew you had someplace to go."

She curled her fingers around his wrist and, turning her lips to his palm, she placed a kiss there. When she returned her gaze to his face, her eyes twinkled mischievously. "You heard Jasper Howard's proposal, didn't you?"

Face coloring hotly, Mangus pulled his hand away and pretended to be adjusting the rudder. "Faith, and it woulda been hard not to." He grinned at her twitching lips. "Could ya not have left the man with some measure of pride?"

Affronted, Adrella rounded on her father. "Pride? *Pride?* And what about me own pride? If you heard the whole conversation, why didn't you march in and knock the man down?"

"Now, Drell," he teased. "Would that have been the Christian thing to do? Besides, you didn't give me time. I thought you handled the matter rather well yourself without me interfering."

Adrella struggled with her growing irascibility. It rather hurt her that her father hadn't done something, *anything,* to Mr. Howard for his supercilious proposal. But he was right. She should have responded in a more Christian way. Paul the Apostle had spoken of a thorn in his side. Well, her Irish temper was hers, and one of these days it was going to land her in a whole peck of trouble.

Her father glanced over her shoulder, and smiled. "There's Dathan."

Adrella turned on her seat and saw Dathan Adams on the parapet surrounding the light at the top of the light-house. He was watching their progress as they crossed the water toward the bay side of the island of Cape St. George, his sandy-brown hair blowing about his head in the growing winds. When he judged them close enough, he disappeared from their view and Adrella knew that he was descending the interior of the tall structure. It would take some time for him to cross the mile distance to reach the pier.

She had taken special care with her appearance today knowing that she was making the trip with her father to deliver Dathan's supplies. Although she knew she would never be considered lovely, she rather felt that the emerald green of her princess-style dress brought out the color in her eyes. Not that she thought she had a hope of attracting a man like Dathan. Not that she even wanted to for that matter. Why should she try to impress a man who barely acknowledged her existence? Why, indeed, she asked her-self in irritation.

When she had met her father at the pier in Apalachic-ola that morning, his lifted eyebrow had caused the color to rush to her face. He said nothing, though, and she was thankful for his silence, although his slight smirk spoke more loudly than any words he could have uttered.

What was there about Dathan that made her normally level head seem more like a seesaw? At times she disliked him intensely, at others, well... He was handsome enough, that was for sure, but it wasn't just his good looks. There was something decidedly mysterious about Dathan Adams. Something that intrigued her.

He and her father had struck up a friendship two years

before when Dathan had first come to their store to purchase supplies. Although he was always courteous, he usually had very little to say to her. Still, whenever she was in close proximity to him, she felt like a clumsy schoolgirl instead of a levelheaded twenty-year-old. It was rather disconcerting.

Swallowing hard, Adrella kept watching until Dathan's broad-shouldered form appeared above the towering sand dunes. Every time she saw Dathan, her heart did funny little flip-flops. She wasn't certain if it was because of his cool gray eyes, or because he was usually so unfriendly toward her. She refused to recognize that it could be anything else.

He reached the pier at the same time their skiff pulled up to it. Mangus threw him the mooring line, and with one swift flip of his wrist, Dathan had it secured.

Dathan's eyes rested momentarily on Adrella before he smiled at her father. "Mangus. I didn't expect to see you today."

That was one of the things that had always impressed Adrella. Dathan's voice was as smooth as butter. Deep and throaty. It never failed to send little skitters along her nerve endings.

Mangus returned his smile. "'Tis my regular day, Dathan."

Glancing about at the incoming cirrus clouds, Dathan nodded. "Aye, but there's a squall brewing. I thought you might wait it out."

Mangus's face grew serious as he joined with Dathan studying the sky. "I'm afraid it's more than just a squall, Dathan. It looks more like a full-fledged hurricane a brewin'. There's a feel to the gulf today that I've felt only a few times before."

Adrella felt her heart plunge to her stomach. Her father

could read the weather better than any man she knew. A hurricane? Why hadn't her father said something earlier? Now she, too, noticed the strange mood of the gulf, the normally blue-green water turning gray and angry.

"I'll help you get the supplies up to the house, but then I'm afraid we're going to have to leave. There won't be any visitin' today."

Dathan nodded, reaching for Adrella's hand to help her from the skiff. "I understand. If you would rather, just pile the things here and I'll get them up to the house."

Mangus was already shaking his head. "No, that won't be necessary. Besides, the rain looks like it's still a few hours away yet. It'll take no time at all to help you with the supplies."

"As you wish." Dathan turned his attention to Adrella. "Adrella, you know where everything's kept. Could you make us a fresh pot of coffee?"

Unable to keep from flushing under his regard, Adrella nodded and hastily moved toward the keeper's cottage. If he noticed her changed attire, he showed no sign of it. Feeling slightly disappointed, Adrella sighed.

"Aye. I'll go ahead and get it started."

As she crossed the beach, Adrella wondered for the hundredth time how a man like Dathan happened to become keeper of the light here at Cape St. George lighthouse. He looked more like someone who would grace a fancy drawing room in England. Although her father had been delivering supplies to him for some time, Adrella still knew very little about Dathan. Every time the past was mentioned, he shied away from discussing it like a frightened colt.

When she reached the small cottage the keepers used, she took the time to look around her at the awe-inspiring view. Miles of ocean met her gaze, the shimmering water rippling from the intensifying wind. Gulls screeched overhead as they searched for food among the tumbling waves. Before long they would disappear to some perch, safe from the fast—approaching storm.

The palm trees and live oaks that surrounded the area were already swaying a rhythm to the gusting wind. The usually raucous sounds of the many birds that wintered here were eerily absent. They had obviously sought shelter on the mainland eight miles away instead of hunkering down here, a sure indication that the weather was going to be rough.

The cirrus clouds of the hurricane's rain bands were drawing closer, their feathery fingers deceptively peaceful against the cobalt-blue sky. Only the wind and waves gave any indication of the gathering storm.

Adrella went in through the kitchen, leaving the door open behind her to allow in the cooling breeze.

She stood staring around at the immaculate room. That was another thing that always surprised her about Dathan. He kept his house as clean and neat as he kept himself. He was a well-organized man, as well. She couldn't remember a time when he had ever been caught unaware. He always had his list ready for her father, and he never seemed to run out of supplies like many of the other keepers.

Normally the keepers came to the mainland for their own supplies, choosing to be able to spend some time with other people. Dathan was different, and her father was always glad to render him service. The two had developed a friendship between them that surprised many. They were so completely opposite. Whereas her father was friendly and open with everyone he met, Dathan was reserved and quiet. He reminded her of the approaching storm, calm and peaceful on the outside but full of fury on the inside. She could see the banked fires in his eyes when he thought no one was looking.

She had been to this house so many times with supplies, she knew where every item in the kitchen was stored. The blue tin coffeepot was already on the stove keeping warm, but Adrella found a pot holder and lifted it to carry outside and dump out the back door in the small garden that Dathan kept close to the house. Rinsing out the pot, she added fresh grounds from the canister and set the pot back on the stove to percolate.

Almost an hour later her father and Dathan arrived with the first load of supplies. Since they usually unloaded the skiff of all supplies before moving up the beach to the cottage, Adrella knew their time would be short. Mangus rubbed his hands together, grinning at his daughter.

"I'm ready for some of that coffee now, Drella me darlin'."

Dathan said nothing, his dark gaze fastening on Adrella hovering over the stove. She poured a cup for her father, then handed one to him, her hands shaking slightly. Irritated with herself, she hid the telltale sign of her nervousness by shoving her hands into the pockets on her apron.

"I think Da's right," she told Dathan. "It looks like a hurricane moving in."

Dathan nodded, sipping his steaming coffee. "I know. It's odd to have one this late in the season, but not unheard of. You two better go ahead and get going before the water gets any rougher. I can bring up the rest of the supplies."

Mangus looked skeptical. "Are you sure, lad? I'll be happy to help."

"I'm sure. Thanks for helping me unload them to the dock."

Shrugging, Mangus finished his coffee and set the cup on the table. "Then we'd best be on our way."

Adrella was conscious of Dathan moving close behind her as they made the mile-long trek back through the path in the woods that separated the light tower from the dock. His presence left her, as always, feeling uncomfortable. The hair prickled on the back of her neck and she reached up to gently rub the spot. Every time she was around Dathan, her nerves seemed to tingle with a life of their own.

The surrounding forest seemed to offer little respite from the fast-approaching gale. Except for the wind, an uncanny stillness settled around them causing them to hurry onward.

When they reached the pier her father helped her into the skiff and turned to shake hands with Dathan. "I'll see you on my next trip out. You have a new list?"

Dathan reached into his pocket, grinning. "Right here."

Mangus took the slip of paper from him, glancing at it briefly. Pocketing it, he nodded his head and then climbed aboard the skiff. "Well, that's it then. God be with you, Dathan."

"And you," Dathan returned softly before untying the mooring line.

The skiff bobbed ever faster as it moved away from the dock. Dathan lifted a keg of flour onto his shoulder and turned to watch their progress. When he was sure they were well away from the surrounding rocks and sandbars, he made his way back to his cottage.

Adding the keg to the pantry in the kitchen, he strolled back to the dock to watch the little skiff move across the water. The wind blew his hair into a riot of confusion, but he didn't object. He lifted his face to the sky, closing his eyes and relishing the power of the zephyr.

When he opened them again, he noticed the skiff floundering amidst the increasing winds. He could make out only one figure on the boat waving frantically in his direction.

Feeling a sudden chill pass over him, Dathan ran back to the house and grabbed his binoculars from a peg on the wall. Hurrying back, he focused them on the boat.

Adrella materialized as he focused the lens. Her terrified face appeared for a moment and then disappeared when she bent to the deck. Heart pounding in alarm, Dathan began running toward his small boat tied to the edge of the dock.

Unmooring it, he pushed out into the turbulent water. His muscles strained against the oars as he rowed closer to the skiff. It seemed for every move he made forward, the waves pushed him two in retreat. In the two years he had lived here he had never seen the gulf in such a temper.

Gritting his teeth with determination, he finally managed to get close enough to throw Adrella a line. She used the rope to pull him closer, tears raining down her cheeks.

When he was close enough, Dathan jumped aboard. "What's happened?" he yelled above the rising wind.

"Da!"

She pointed to where her father lay clutching his chest, sprawled on the floor of the skiff. Moving quickly to his side, Dathan knelt beside him and felt for a pulse. It moved weakly against his fingers. Lifting the lid of one eye, he took note of the lack of response to the light. Dathan swallowed hard, his heart lodging somewhere close to his throat. The cold clammy skin and blue-veined hands were not reassuring.

He looked up at Adrella, his gray eyes dark with worry. "We have to get you back to the house."

"But Da needs the doctor! We can't go back!"

Looking around at the swelling waves, Dathan shook his head. "We're not close enough to the mainland and the wind and waves are too fierce. We'll never make it eight miles in this wind. The house is the best bet."

Adrella bit her lip in indecision. Not waiting for an answer, Dathan moved to the oars and began to turn the skiff back toward the island.

Dropping to her knees, Adrella began to talk to her father. "Hang on, Da. Hang on!" she told him, pushing the soggy hair from his eyes. Her voice became desperate "Don't you dare die on me!"

Terror clutching at her heart, Adrella began to petition the Lord on her father's behalf. She pled fervently for his life, while with fierce concentration Dathan struggled against the turbulent waves.

"If you've a mind, you can grab that extra set of oars and give a hand," he yelled.

Adrella knew from the tone of his voice that Dathan was not making a suggestion. Reluctant to leave her father's side, but knowing the feasibility of making it to shore more swiftly with two rowers, Adrella grabbed the other set of oars and added her own power to that of the man fighting against the ferocity of the increasing wind.

It seemed to take forever for them to reach the shore. Dathan quickly jumped from the boat, tying it to the small dock with the mooring line.

Setting Adrella to the side, he gently lifted Mangus into his arms. Even at such a time as this, Adrella couldn't help but be impressed with the power of the man. His muscles bulged against the older man's weight, yet he lifted him with ease.

Dathan didn't wait to see if Adrella followed. Piqued, she lifted her skirts and hurried after him.

Chapter 2

Adrella was scarcely aware of time passing. Dathan came and went, but her attention was riveted on her father lying on Dathan's bed. Mangus hadn't yet awakened from his attack, and Adrella felt dread turn her stomach into a tight knot. If anything should happen to her father...well, the idea didn't bear thinking about.

She set the rocking chair she was in to rocking, the back-and-forth rhythm somewhat soothing. She looked around her noting the Spartan furnishings of the bedroom. The one spot of color in the room was the beautiful quilt now covering her father's still form. There had to be a story behind that quilt, she was sure of it. It seemed so out of place here among the rustic furniture.

Two small daguerreotypes were sitting on the dresser. One was of a man who looked very much like Dathan. He was in a Union uniform, his unsmiling face a decided contradiction to the eyes so full of life that they could almost see right through you. The other picture was of a man and woman dressed more elegantly than anything she had ever seen. She stared at the pictures blankly. At any other time her curiosity would have made her question Dathan on the people, but now she couldn't bring herself to be interested enough to care.

Sighing, she turned her attention back to her father. The whiteness of his face filled her with dread. He seemed to have aged in just hours. She reached across and pushed his graying hair back from his forehead. If prayers could save someone's life, then her father would open his eyes and smile at her soon because she had been storming heaven since her father had first crumpled to the floor of the skiff in a seemingly lifeless heap.

Dathan quietly entered the room. He gave Adrella one cursory glance before giving Mangus his full attention. Adrella was surprised when Dathan put an instrument against her father's chest, and held the other end to his ear.

"What are you doing?" she asked in alarm.

Dathan's eyes never left her father. "I'm checking his heart."

Adrella's look went from Dathan to her father, and then back again. She recognized the instrument that Dr. Taylor sometimes used to check a person's heart. Why would Dathan think he needed to check her father's heart?

"Is it… Will he…?" she stopped, unable to continue.

Heaving a great sigh, Dathan turned sympathetic eyes her way. Their cloudy gray reminded her of the ever encroaching storm outside.

"Adrella, your father's condition is not good."

Panic robbed her of speech momentarily. How could Dathan possibly know such a thing? Her anger grew to unreasonable bounds as the fear of losing her father almost consumed her.

"I told you we needed to see the doctor! Dr. Taylor could have helped."

Dathan shook his head, folding his stethoscope and placing it on the table beside the bed. "No. The good doctor couldn't have done anything. There's nothing that *can* be done," he told her, his voice thick with frustration.

It took a moment for his words to sink in, but when they did Adrella quickly rose to her feet.

"He's dying?" she choked.

"Yes. He is." Although his words were clipped and cold, there was pity and anguish in his expression.

Her green eyes grew large, moving restlessly from her father to Dathan. It was too much to comprehend. She felt as though she were drifting on a surging tide. Her tiny voice lacked conviction.

"He can't die."

"Adrella…"

"No!" Backing away from Dathan, she dropped to her father's side. "No, I don't believe you! You're no doctor. What do you know? We need to get him to the mainland. To Doc Taylor."

Going to the window, Dathan jerked back the dark drapes. It looked like dusk outside, and while they watched, the first spattering of raindrops hit the glass.

"We would never make it. The sea is too rough, and the winds have grown fierce."

A lone tear slid down Adrella's white cheek. "We should have gone earlier," she accused.

"Adrella…" Dathan pressed his lips together. "I *am* a doctor."

Adrella's lips parted in surprise. Several seconds ticked by before she could speak.

"You? A doctor?"

"Yes. Trust me when I tell you that there is nothing that could have been done."

Adrella was totally confused. Why would a doctor be out here on an isolated island pretending to be a lighthouse keeper? Her thoughts must have shown on her face, for Dathan's expression once again became closed.

"I have duties to perform. I'll check in with you later. There's nothing that can be done for him right now except to make him as comfortable as can be." He hesitated. "If you need me, just call."

When he turned to leave the room, Adrella quickly rose to her feet and clutched his arm. Her pain-filled eyes meshed with his.

"How long?"

For a moment she thought he wouldn't answer her, but then he took a deep breath and looked her squarely in the face.

"I don't know. It could be hours. It could be days."

Adrella's heart sank. Hours? She might have only a few precious hours with her father?

"I'm sorry," Dathan told her, and she had never heard his voice so soft. It wrapped around her, warm and comforting, helping to ease the chill of her despondency. Nodding her head, she brushed the tears from her cheeks and turned back to the bed.

Dathan hesitated in the doorway, but there was really nothing more he could say or do. Besides, he had his duties to perform. If this storm was as bad as he feared, any ship on the water, if it survived the savage sea, would need his guiding light.

Noticing the tears running in a silent stream down Adrella's cheeks, he felt a tight knot form in his stomach. He pulled a handkerchief from his pocket and handed it to her, watching as she struggled to hold back the tide of her grief. Gritting his teeth, he left her alone with her sorrow.

Leaving the cottage, he stopped to take inventory of the surrounding gulf. Already the water had risen higher against the shore. Lifting his face to the sky, he prayed for protection for them all, and although he really doubted it would do any good, he prayed for Mangus as well.

His heart ached for the loss of his friend. Mangus had broken through the tough shell Dathan had erected around himself and offered his friendship. Now it was hard to remember a time when the older man hadn't been a part of his life, his godly attitude shaming Dathan into an awareness of his own shortcomings.

Many an afternoon after delivering supplies, he would play chess with Dathan and share stories. The older man had seen more than his share of heartache having lost a wife and son in childbirth, yet he never seemed to lose his zest for life.

Dathan smiled slightly, battling through the fierce wind. Mangus would have loved this storm. Stopping momentarily, Dathan shook his head to clear it of such futile thinking. Mangus wasn't gone from this earth yet, and there was always the possibility that God would take pity and intervene. And yet all common sense told him there was no hope. Adrella would be devastated if her father died.

When he reached the lighthouse, Dathan had to heave against the wind to open the door leading into the interior. He finally managed to get the door closed, the sudden darkness engulfing him, the storm sounding much farther away. Taking the lamp from inside the doorway, Dathan lit it and climbed the dark circular stairway to the top of the light. When he reached the top, he took a moment to look about him. As always, the sight filled him with awe and a greater appreciation for the One who had created the surrounding landscape.

Through the glass windows housing the light, he could see outside, the sea tumbling about with rising fury. The churning waters seemed to grow angrier as he watched.

With the darkness of the storm overshadowing the sunlight, he knew he would have to light the lamps early. Although this light had only a third-order Fresnel lens, it would still penetrate far out into the murky gulf. In good conditions the light would shine over fifteen miles, but then these weren't exactly good conditions. He hoped the dark angle that had been created by damage to the lens during the War Between the States wouldn't be a problem.

As was required by the Lighthouse Board, he had already prepared the lamps early this morning. All that remained to do was to light them. That done, Dathan stared into the glowing lamp, his thoughts with a brokenhearted girl watching her father slowly die. Slamming his palms against the iron railing, he gritted his teeth, furious over his inability to do more for his friend. If only he had gotten to him sooner. If only he hadn't taken the time to go back for his binoculars. If… If… If… There was no use thinking about what was in the past; he had more pressing problems taking place in the present.

Maybe someday in the future there would be ways to deal with such cases, but as for now, all he could do was watch as his friend slipped slowly away.

It was hard to breathe past the lump that had formed in his throat. He squeezed his eyes shut tightly to deny the tears threatening release. Taking a deep breath, he quickly finished his business and headed back down the stairs.

Pausing at the bottom with his hand on the door latch, he wondered what he would find when he went back to the house. When he stepped outside, the wind hit him with such force he had to struggle to remain upright and in place. Impelling himself forward, he fought his way through the furious winds.

The sea was already inching its way up the sands of the shore. He decided that it would be best to move some of the barrels of lard oil up to the lighthouse just in case the storm was as destructive as he thought it might be. They would be safe in the brick shelter, but he wasn't too certain about the oil house.

After he had struggled to move three drums, he decided he would just have to hope and pray about the rest. There was no more room and he needed to get back to the house.

Entering the kitchen, he removed his wet coat and boots, placing them beside the kitchen door. He padded his way back to the bedroom in his damp socks and found Adrella exactly as he had left her.

"There's no change," she told him dully, frowning at the water dripping from Dathan's hair and face.

That wasn't exactly true, but he decided not to say anything. Already he could hear that the timbre of Mangus's breathing had altered. The slight rattle in his chest warned Dathan that the time was near.

Mangus suddenly opened his eyes. Adrella got up from the floor where she had been kneeling and settled next to him on the bed.

"Da! Oh, thank God."

It took a moment for Mangus to be able to speak. His dull green eyes met Dathan's, and Dathan realized that the older man knew he hadn't much time left.

"Adrella," he wheezed. "I need to speak to Dathan... alone."

Adrella turned surprised eyes Dathan's way. "But, Da..."

Mangus struggled to reach her hand lying next to his on the bed. He squeezed her fingers slightly.

"Please, Drell."

Reluctantly she got up from the bed. Dathan easily read the emotions flashing through her eyes before she turned away.

"I'll be in the kitchen preparing us some tea," she told them, the hurt evident in her voice.

Dathan watched her leave, shutting the door behind her. He turned to Mangus.

"What is it, old friend?" he asked, sitting next to Mangus in the spot Adrella had recently vacated. He took the older man's hand.

Mangus gave a slight squeeze, rough fingers meeting rough fingers. "Dathan," he started, flinching when a sharp pain sliced through his chest. Taking a deep breath, he went on. "I want you to look after Adrella for me."

At Dathan's startled look, Mangus's halting voice continued. "She has…no one else, and…nowhere else to go. I can't die…in peace…until I know she's been taken care of."

Dathan shoved a hand back through his hair. "What exactly are you saying, Mangus?"

"I want you…to marry…Adrella."

Dathan sighed. That's just what he thought the older man was suggesting. He couldn't fault him for wanting what was best for his child, but only at such a time could he ever conceive of Mangus asking such a thing.

"Mangus, you don't know what you're asking."

Mangus gave an imperceptible nod. "Aye, I do. I…trust you, Dathan. Regardless of the man you claim to be…I can see into your heart. You're a good man who loves the Lord."

Rubbing his temple with an agitated hand, Dathan shook his head. How was he going to dissuade his friend from such a thought and yet give him the peace he was seeking?

"You don't know me at all, Mangus. Besides, I have no desire to marry."

A slight smile curled the older man's lips. "You may not realize it, but you *need* each other. You'll be...good for one another."

Dathan's voice lifted slightly. "Look, you old match-maker you, even if I agreed, I'm fairly certain Adrella wouldn't."

"She will if you tell her...it was her da's last wish," he husked, his voice growing softer.

Dathan knew Mangus had only moments left to live. He couldn't allow him to go with worry on his heart. He loved the man too much. He and Adrella would just have to sort this out later.

"I'll do what you ask, Mangus," Dathan told him softly, reluctantly.

The smile increased on the older man's face, the stress lines around his mouth easing, and he closed his eyes. "Thank you, Dathan. God bless."

Dathan was riddled with guilt at his deception but he didn't know what else to do. He had hoped never to be in this position again. The exact reason he had left the medical profession. Too often he had lied to give peace to a dying man, bloody from wounds inflicted by other men. Even then the guilt had gnawed away at him, the helplessness of knowing he could do nothing to give them their last wishes.

Mangus's eyelids slowly lifted. "Now...send me colleen back in here...and let me tell her goodbye."

Adrella leaned against the counter in the kitchen, her thoughts as turbulent as the weather outside.

Why had her da made her leave the room? What had he to say to Dathan that he couldn't say in her presence?

She pushed the coffeepot to the back of the stove and set the kettle to boil for tea. She had no desire for the beverage, but it gave her something to do.

The wind and rain rattled against the panes in the window over the sink. She could hear the shingles being torn from the roof. It wouldn't be long before the rain would penetrate through the bare places. She pulled pans from the cupboard to set up for the ensuing drips.

Time seemed to drag as she waited for some kind of word from the other room.

The kettle began to whistle and she took it off the stove and placed it on a hot pad on the wooden kitchen table. Taking a cup from the cupboard, she poured the steaming water into it and then added the loose tea, all the while wondering what was happening in the next room.

Could it be true that Dathan was really a doctor? Would he be able to do something, *anything,* to help her da? He had said that there was nothing to be done, but surely there was something. Da couldn't die. He just couldn't! What would she do without her da? He was her whole existence.

She added cream to her tea, slowly stirring the contents while straining to hear what was going on in the bedroom. Taking a sip of the hot brew, she felt the warmth spread through and warm her from inside out, yet her heart still felt frozen.

Dathan eventually called and Adrella hurried back into the room. She passed Dathan in the doorway giving him a superficial glance as she went by.

Taking her place on the bed, Adrella took her father's hand and began to rub softly. "Da, I love you," she told him, and the tears she had held back at the first sign of wakefulness now slipped silently down her cheeks in an unceasing river.

"Ah, my little colleen," he breathed softly, lifting his other hand and stroking away the tears. "I love you, too, lass. Now…do your old da a favor."

"Anything, Da."

He held out a shaking hand to her. "Take me wedding ring off me finger."

Adrella's eyes widened in surprise. "No, Da. You have never taken off your ring. It belongs to you. It will be…" She didn't finish the sentence, for it hinted of her acceptance of the inevitable. She had been about to say that it would be buried with him.

For a second Mangus's eyes flashed fire. "I said take it," he said, his voice weak but still full of command.

Used to obeying, Adrella did as he asked. She carefully slid it from his large finger, curling her hand around the warm gold metal.

"It's for your husband," he rattled. "I've taken care of everything else, now this is for you. You and…"

Adrella saw her father's eyes grow wide as he stared past her shoulder. Turning, she saw nothing there.

"Faith," Mangus's voice filled the room with awe. "I can see them."

Dathan and Adrella exchanged worried glances.

"Who? Who do you see, Da?"

"They're beautiful," he intoned with reverence. He smiled, nodding his head. "Aye, I'm ready."

"No!" Adrella clutched his hands tightly. "No, Da. Don't leave me!"

Mangus turned blank eyes to Adrella. "Goodbye, me little girl," he breathed softly.

His eyes fluttered closed, his breath expired on a slow sigh and he was gone.

* * *

The little house creaked and groaned as the wind intensified. The panes of glass continued to shake in their frames.

Dathan stared out the window, his thoughts far away. He had always been a man of his word, and now he had promised to care for Adrella. The thought discomfited him.

"Here's your tea."

He turned to find Adrella setting his cup on the table, her tear-drenched features leaving her wan, the freckles standing out prominently against her white face. He had always considered her to be a rather plain little thing, but now she looked positively homely. There was nothing about her looks that would instantly snag a man's attention, and yet he couldn't think of anyone he would rather be stranded with at such a time.

"Thanks."

He seated himself across from her, turning the cup round and round in its saucer. His eyes lifted to her, and he found her watching him.

"What did me da mean when he said he had arranged everything?" she asked dully.

He noticed that she had placed her father's wedding band on her thumb. He smiled slightly, noting that it was even too large for that appendage. Somehow he didn't think now was the time to discuss it. He had some decisions to make quickly, and he was afraid that Adrella wasn't going to like some of them.

"We can discuss that later," he told her softly. "Right now, I think we need to make preparations to move to the lighthouse."

"Why?" she asked him, the surprise evident in her voice.

His brow furrowed in consternation and he stared into

the contents of his cup as though it held the answer to all the questions churning through his mind. He couldn't bring himself to look at her because he knew she was going to balk at what he had to say.

The kitchen window was shaken by another gust of wind, the rain peppering against it in an ever-increasing downpour. Dathan tensed.

"The gulf is much higher than I have ever seen it. I'm afraid when the eyewall hits, the storm surge is going to cover this house."

Shocked, Adrella stared at him, her lips parted slightly. If anything, her face grew more ashen. "What will we do?"

"We need to take some supplies and move them to the top of the light tower."

Biting her bottom lip, her glance went to the back bedroom. "What about Da?"

Dathan took a deep breath, fixing Adrella with a steely look. "If I have time, I will wrap the body and take it with us."

"If you have time!" she choked. "Well, I won't leave without him."

"Adrella." He tried to reason with her. "I have never seen a storm of such magnitude. Parts of the outbuilding are already being damaged, as well as this house. If this storm is as destructive as I think it's going to be, we could be in for a long period of confinement."

"I don't care! I want to bury me da with a proper funeral!" she said in desperation.

"It may not be possible," he argued. "The heat and humidity could cause the body to decompose rapidly. It wouldn't be very pleasant."

Adrella slumped down in her chair. Such thoughts were beyond her right now. It was hard enough to take in that her father had died, much less talking about decomposing bodies. She gave a little sniff.

"I need your help," Dathan told her, jerking her thoughts to the present.

His words registered, but her mind was too numb to comprehend them for several seconds. She hesitated but a moment before getting slowly to her feet. "What do you need me to do?"

She saw surprise flash briefly through his eyes as she struggled to maintain a composure that was fast disintegrating. She was Mangus Murphy's daughter; she would not fall apart when she was needed most.

"I think we'll only have time for one trip," he told her quietly. "I've bagged as much as I can of the supplies, but we'll need to take them together."

If there was only time for one trip, then by default he was saying that they couldn't take her father with them. Could she really bring herself to leave him?

As Adrella stood hesitating, a heavy burst of wind shook the house sending a piece of debris crashing through the kitchen window. Adrella screamed, and Dathan jumped to his feet.

The wind and rain blew in through the broken pane, whistling eerily through the room.

"We have to go *now*," he told her. He grabbed his dripping Macintosh from beside the door and helped Adrella put it on. The garment, made for a man, swallowed her whole.

Handing Adrella the smaller sack, he told her roughly, "Stay behind me. Hold on to my belt, and whatever you do, don't let go."

He opened the door and it slammed inward with the force of the wind. Taking a deep breath, Dathan plunged outside, dragging Adrella along behind him.

They fought their way through the storm, the winds making any debris a lethal weapon. Had they waited any longer, they would have never made it past the front yard. Already the churning gulf waters were lapping at the base of the towering light.

Although Adrella was somewhat protected from the pelting rain by the India Rubber coat, it hit Dathan with increasing ferocity. They were blinded by the pounding fury of the drenching rain and hurricane-force winds. Dathan held up an arm to protect his face from the onslaught.

He found his way unerringly to the huge stone edifice of the light. He dragged Adrella inside, fighting to shut the door behind them.

Both were panting with the exertion. Adrella bent over to get her breath, her sides heaving with the effort. "What about…what about Da?"

There was dread in Dathan's voice when he answered her. "It's too late. I can't go back outside."

Adrella jerked her head up to argue, but stopped short at the sight of the blood on Dathan's face. Her eyes widened in surprise.

"What happened?"

Dathan dotted a finger against the dripping blood. "The pebbles are like bullets," he told her in awe. "I've never seen anything like this." He took the lantern he had left lit and began to climb the stairs to the top. "Come on. It'll be safer farther up."

Adrella followed slowly, her strength already exhausted. She glanced at the whitewashed stone walls surrounding her, so close it felt as though they were closing in. She sat down on the stairs, and pushed her palms against her eyes. Her father's burial lay heavily on her mind.

Dathan brought the light back to her. "What is it?"

"Da," she answered dully.

Eyes dark with compassion, Dathan sat down next to her on the steps.

"Adrella, your father loved the sea. If something does happen, and the island is flooded…"

She turned to him slowly, catching his unspoken message. "A burial at sea?"

He shrugged, not knowing what else to say.

"Is there no way?" she asked him, her bottom lip trembling.

Dathan lifted the lantern higher to push back the darkness. Adrella heard his swiftly indrawn breath.

"What is it?" she asked fearfully.

Dathan motioned with his free hand to the floor below. Water was pouring rapidly through the small bottom window aperture in the wall. Since the window was several feet off the ground, it gave Adrella and Dathan an idea of how far the gulf had risen with the storm tides.

Adrella scrambled upward on the iron stairs, bumping into Dathan. Terror filled eyes lifted to his face. He met her look with one of extreme resolution.

"There's no going back now."

Chapter 3

All the rest of the day Dathan and Adrella clung to their perch in the lighthouse tower. They divided the food between them when either, or both, got hungry, which wasn't very often. The howling wind outside and the rising water level below them robbed them of much of their appetite. That and not knowing what was happening to the world outside. To Mangus's body, more precisely.

Periodically throughout the day, the lighthouse would shake when some large object was hurled into its side by the fierce wind, but the brick tower held. It was terrifying to think that something large enough to rattle the lighthouse could be thrown about by a mere wind.

During the long hours Dathan tended the light. Normally the light would be cared for in the morning and lit in the evening but the storm made it necessary to keep the light burning continuously. Adrella pitied any of the men aboard ships that were caught in this gale.

Fortunately Dathan had been able to move several drums of oil farther up the stairway out of the rising flood-water. The others sat on the floor of the lighthouse, buried beneath at least ten feet of water, along with the door to the outside world. There was no way he could reach the oil house to get more, if there was still an oil house left.

She had offered to help Dathan, but there was nothing she could really do. Often she was merely in the way. He never said so, but she could tell.

Dathan sat down on the step above her head, interrupting Adrella's pensive musings.

"Well there's one good thing about this storm. It keeps the mosquitoes away," he told her, the seriousness of his eyes belying his cheerful voice.

Adrella barely acknowledged his words. The air in the tower had grown stale, but there was no way to really relieve them of their problem short of going outside. And *that* was out of the question. The wind was still sending debris flying, making it a lethal projection. Frankly, to be free of the tower, she would have welcomed even those horrendous little pests.

Dathan shifted slightly, bringing Adrella's attention around to him. He was studying her as though she were a bug under a microscope. She felt the color rise to her cheeks. She could only imagine what she must look like, and even then, she was afraid her imagination wouldn't do it justice. Her hair had always looked like a frizzy mess whenever it got wet and tangled, and the dress she had been so proud of now hung limply on her tired body.

Although Dathan had gone through the same things she had, he wasn't nearly as disheveled. In fact he looked as handsome as ever, even with the small cuts on his face from flying objects.

Her look was suddenly caught by dimples peeking forth

when he gave her one of his rare smiles. Their eyes met and the smile slowly slid from his face. He glanced away, releasing her from the spell his intense look had generated. They once again retreated into a morose silence.

After a time the winds seemed to stop as suddenly as they had arrived. Adrella fearfully listened for the sound of rain, but everything was unusually quiet.

"The eye," she pronounced solemnly.

Dathan lifted his head, listening as well. "You're right. The worst should be over. As the eyewall moves over land it should diminish in intensity. I'm afraid, though, that we still have a lot more rain to come."

Adrella knew he was right. Having lived in Florida for the past several years, hurricanes were no new thing to her. But there had never been one of this intensity.

"Do you think I could go up to the parapet?"

Dathan started to get up, but she placed a restraining hand on his shoulder.

"Alone," she told him, her face coloring hotly. He stared at her as though she had suddenly grown horns. She could read the thoughts flashing across his countenance and re-alized the exact moment he knew what she was asking.

"Ah. Of course. I'll wait and go up after you."

Adrella climbed the stairs and pushed her way through the small door leading to the outside. She had needed to relieve herself for some time now, but the thought of doing so was embarrassing. She had been hoping against hope that they would be free from the lighthouse a lot sooner than she now realized they would.

Night had fallen. Pinpricks of light spangled the dark sky through the break in the storm clouds. There was no moon to see by so she could not tell if the keeper's house was still standing. She could still hear water lapping against the side of the lighthouse. She finished what she needed to do and hurried below to tell Dathan.

"How do you think Apalachicola fared?" she asked after Dathan had returned.

Apalachicola was situated close to the water. Most of the people in Apalach, as the locals called it, made their living oystering and shrimping. Before the War Between the States cotton had been king, but the blockades had put a stop to that. Although their town had weathered many storms in the past there had been nothing of this magnitude.

Dathan shrugged. "I hate to think," he told her, his voice darkly foreboding.

They fell into an uncomfortable silence. That's how it had been all day. Silence, with intermittent spurts of conversation. That they were both uncomfortable with the situation was obvious, but Adrella had the feeling that there was something more than the storm on Dathan's mind. She wondered if it had anything to do with her father's parting words. She turned to ask him but Dathan was already climbing the tower stairs once again, his broad back as imposing as the stone structure they were protected by.

Glancing down at her hand, she curled her thumb around her father's wedding band. Looking at it now brought a lump to her throat. Her father had never taken the ring from his finger, even after being fifteen years a widower. How could such a love last so long beyond the grave?

Her gaze went to Dathan at the top of the stairway where he was tending the light. Dathan was very much like her own da, every bit the gentleman. The thought brought her a small measure of comfort. She knew without a doubt that she was completely safe with him.

She laid her head against the stair above her, shifting as

she grew more uncomfortable. There was really no way to relax sitting on these cold metal steps. She sighed wearily. She was so very tired, drained physically as well as emotionally, but it was impossible to rest. For several hours her only respite had been intermittent periods of sleep sitting up against the stairway. The position was just too annoying to allow a restful sleep. Hour after dreary hour passed without any relief.

Dathan came and sat next to her. Reaching out, he pulled her into the crook of his arm while he leaned back against the rail. She lifted her face to his in surprise. When he bent to look at her, his face was mere inches from her own.

"Try to get some sleep," he told her huskily. "I know it's not very comfortable, but it's the best I can do."

Adrella swallowed hard. "What…what about you?"

"I'm fine. Go to sleep, Adrella."

Surprisingly, she did.

Dathan watched Adrella sleep, smiling at her soft snore. He knew she was exhausted, not only from struggling against the storm, but also the overwhelming grief of losing a loved one. As a doctor, he knew that sleep was the best thing for her right now.

He shifted slightly so that he could reach the small Bible he always kept in his back pocket. The book was wet, its pages wrinkled, yet still readable. He carefully handled the sodden pages looking for some form of comfort. The scriptures had never failed him in this capacity and he knew they wouldn't now.

Carefully flipping the soggy pages, he sought the book of Psalms. In the fifth verse of the thirtieth chapter he found what he was looking for. "For His anger endureth but a moment; in His favor is life: weeping may endure for a night, but joy cometh in the morning."

That was something his father had always told him: no matter what happens, there's always tomorrow.

Even for Mangus that was true. When Mangus next opened his eyes he would begin a new day, a day that would never end.

Sorrow was for those left behind.

He glanced down at Adrella and felt a sudden, overwhelming sense of duty. Mangus had trusted him with his most precious possession. The thought brought a tightness to his throat. What had Mangus seen in him to make Mangus believe so highly in his ability to care for his daughter? Whatever it was, he knew he couldn't let the man down.

Adrella was nothing much to look at, but she had a heart as big as the gulf. Still, those freckles were rather endearing. His lips curled into a slight smile. And those big green eyes of hers! A man could get lost in those eyes. But heaven help a man when they flashed green fire!

What was he to do? Did caring for her necessarily mean tying himself to her for life? No matter how he tried to justify it, he knew with certainty that he could not turn his back on her. The mantle of responsibility settled heavily across his shoulders. He would care for her as conscientiously as Mangus would have.

He carefully laid the small Bible on the metal stairs to dry and pulled Adrella closer. Before long he nodded off to sleep.

When Adrella awakened toward morning, she felt much refreshed, although disheveled and dirty. She smiled wryly. There was all that water below her, and still no way to take a proper bath.

She turned her head slightly on Dathan's chest and

found his eyes closed, his mouth slightly parted as he gently snored. Her smile turned into a grin, and she refrained from movement in case she awakened him. She studied his features a long time, noting the firm chin now covered with a day's growth. The smile slowly slid from her face as her look drifted down to wander over his broad shoulders and then to where his arms lightly encircled her waist. He looked very much as she had always pictured a pirate. She hastily reined in her wayward imaginings.

Suddenly his eyes opened, still fuzzy with sleep, and he was looking directly into her own eyes. It amazed Adrella how fast his eyes went from cloudy with sleep, to razor sharp and fully awake. She sat up, disentangling herself from his hold and pushing her straggly hair from her face. Embarrassed by her thoughts, she couldn't bring herself to look at him.

Dathan rose swiftly to his feet, brushing down his clothes. He bent down and picked up a small Bible that was lying on the steps. Adrella knew he was watching her, but she was too shy to look up.

"The wind is slackening off, I think," he told her. "The water should start to recede soon, then we can get out of here."

For the first time Adrella wasn't so certain that she wanted to. It terrified her to think of what she might find beyond this stone fortress. It had become a safe haven over the past day.

She was certain that devastation awaited their return to the outside world. Although she had continually prayed that the floodwaters had not reached the keeper's house, she had little faith that those prayers had been answered. Frankly, she was beginning to doubt that *any* of her prayers would be answered.

Dathan held out his hand to her. "If you don't mind getting a little wet, you can come up to the parapet and get some fresh air."

Thrilled with the idea, Adrella quickly placed her hand into his. "I'd love some fresh air. What's a little water anyway?"

Adrella followed Dathan up the metal stairs. When he reached the top, he lifted the hatch door to allow her access to the parapet surrounding the light.

She climbed through the small hole and was immediately hit by pellets of rain, though the droplets no longer stung when they found open skin.

Adrella took a deep breath, reveling in the fresh scent of rain-drenched air. She forced her heart to still its rapid beating, but found it impossible when Dathan came to stand behind her.

Looking out over the gray landscape, it was still hard to see anything beyond several feet, for although they were on the receding side of the hurricane, the rain was torrential. She tried to see past the tower to the keeper's cottage, but was unable to distinguish anything through the rain and gloom of approaching day.

"Can you see the cottage?" she asked Dathan without turning around.

He leaned over her shoulder, and she was pushed precariously near the railing. Feeling her tense, Dathan took her by the shoulders and moved her out of his way. Her shoulders tingled from the brief contact.

He peered through the falling water for a long time before he finally shook his head regretfully. "I still can't see a thing."

They stood together looking out at the receding storm. Another day should see an end to the rain. Neither one said anything, each busy with their own thoughts. Before long they were soaked.

"We'd better get back inside," Dathan remarked, "before we wind up with pneumonia."

Adrella was reluctant to return to the stuffy confines of the tower, but she knew he was right. Though the temperatures were still fairly warm, their wet clothing would give them a chill.

"Let's go into the lamp room," Dathan told her, leading her to the door that opened into the small chamber. "The heat from the lamp will help dry our clothes."

The confines of the space were even more claustrophobic than the tower. Never having liked close quarters, Adrella struggled to keep her mind off the tight feeling in her chest. Well she could remember the ship ride from Ireland so many years ago, and the small areas allowed to the passengers. Ever since, she had been unable to breathe inside a tight place.

Still, the air here smelled of burning oil and wax, and while it was not altogether pleasant, it was far better than the dank smell of the sea water in the tower.

Her gaze settled on Dathan as he adjusted the light and polished the lens. He was such an enigma. She found herself wanting to know more about him.

"Dathan," she asked. "Why do you call yourself a doctor?"

She saw his shoulders tense. "Because I am."

She considered him quietly. It was quite obvious that this was something he didn't wish to discuss. "Are or was?"

At first she thought he wouldn't answer her, but then he settled an impatient glare upon her. "I was a doctor in the Union army," he answered stiffly.

Puzzled, Adrella cocked her head and continued to examine him. "How did you come to be a lighthouse keeper then?"

Sighing, Dathan lifted his eyes briefly to the ceiling.

Turning, he fixed her with a compelling look. His gaze roved her features briefly.

"I was a doctor up until, and during, the War Between the States."

Her forehead puckered. "But not now?"

"No, not now." Picking up a rag, he began to polish an already sparkling lens. "I gave it up."

There was such finality in his voice that Adrella knew that he wanted to end the conversation, but she found herself more curious than ever.

"Gave it up?"

He pushed his lips outward before turning and fixing her with an eloquent eye. "Let's just say that I got over the feeling that I needed to help my fellow man."

She knew she should leave it alone, but she was intrigued. Dathan could quote the scriptures better than most ministers she knew, and she knew he was a godly man. Then how could he not want to help mankind? Something didn't fit right, like a puzzle missing a few pieces.

Adrella studied him intently, a frown puckering her forehead. "Most people give up on God," she said quietly, "but you gave up on mankind instead, didn't you?"

It all made perfect sense to her now. The recent War Between the States had not had as much effect here in Florida as it had in other parts of the country. Still, they had not come out unscathed. They had only this year been allowed back into the Union after the Republicans had gained control of the Florida state government and ratified the Fourteenth Amendment to the Constitution, guaranteeing civil rights.

The war had made a big difference to their way of life in Apalachicola. The blockades, occupation by Union forces—their way of life had been changed, probably forever.

Florida was proud of the fact that of all the Confederate states, only the state capitals of Tallahassee and Austin, Texas hadn't been captured. Although Tallahassee hadn't fallen, it too had not been unscathed.

There hadn't been nearly as much blood shed in Florida as in other parts of the country, but the effects of the war were still there. Those men who left to fight in other parts of the country and then returned to Florida after the war were changed, and often not for the better.

Dathan's dark-eyed look settled on her once again. His eyes were filled with a pain she couldn't begin to understand.

"God isn't responsible for the stupidity of man. I have never blamed Him for the atrocities I saw committed against human beings. Even though people have had the Word of God for eons of time, they still reject the simplicity of His saving grace. His love. All that matters is their petty little differences. Their greed!"

She was surprised at his vehemence. "So you choose to shut yourself off from the rest of the world."

It was not a question, but he answered her anyway.

"Yes. That's exactly what I choose to do."

She wanted to remind him of Jesus's great commission, to seek and save the lost, but she suddenly found herself unable to argue a theological point. Her own faith had undergone a dramatic restructuring since she arrived on the island. She couldn't understand the loss of her father, the possibility of being alone for the rest of her life, the destruction she was certain awaited them just beyond that iron door. Nothing made sense anymore.

Seeming to sense some of what she was feeling, Dathan dropped his rag into the pile next to the door.

"I think we're dry enough, now. Let's go back to the tower."

Sighing, she allowed him to help her back into the tower and down the ladder. She curled her nose slightly at the musty smell, but kept her comments to herself. After all, it was not Dathan's fault that they were stranded here.

Surprisingly, the rain had refreshed Adrella. She felt cleaner than she had since she left her home. If she had a bar of soap, she would march herself back up those stairs and take a proper bath in the rain! Her tangled hair had been softened by the rainwater, and now she settled herself on the steps in the tower and, using her fingers, tried to comb it into some semblance of order.

Dathan sat two steps above her, seeming to watch her ministrations with some interest.

"You have beautiful hair," he complimented.

Adrella's fingers grew clumsy under his watchful regard.

"Thank you."

Silence settled around them, but it was a congenial one. They both had much to think about, but neither one dared to offer their thoughts aloud.

Chapter 4

Adrella watched Dathan wade through the murky water to the iron door. The tight seal of the door had kept the water trapped inside the lighthouse for two long and dreary days after the rain had stopped. Now the water had finally diminished to the bottom of the window, but there was no way for the water below the window to escape except through the entry door.

It took some effort by Dathan to open it, but finally he was able to swing it a crack and the trapped water rushed out and spread over the already drenched sand outside.

Adrella released her breath slowly, thankful to be able to finally leave the safe, but claustrophobic, haven of the tower, but reluctant to see what lay on the other side.

Dathan seemed to have no such compunctions. Without waiting for her, he quickly exited the structure and disappeared from her view.

When Adrella joined him outside, she was unprepared

for the sight that met her eyes. There was nothing left of the lightkeeper buildings except pieces of scattered debris and the badly damaged brick chimney of the main house. In fact, the whole island seemed to be littered with wreckage. Tree limbs had been snapped from the surrounding woods and were strewn across their path. It looked like the entire island had been bombed with heavy artillery fire.

"Goodness," Adrella exclaimed softly. She crossed to where Dathan was standing, his face grim as he studied the area about him. Apparently without thinking, he clasped her hand and pulled her with him.

"Come on. Let's see if we can find...Mangus."

Although they searched the island as completely as they could, by the time night began to fall there was no sign of the body. Adrella felt her heart twist painfully, and giving a little sob, she sank to the wet sand.

Sighing, Dathan turned toward her.

"I'm sorry," he told her softly. "I should have gone back for his body."

Adrella shook her head. "You couldn't. You would have been killed." She lifted sad eyes to his face. "It's all right, Dathan. I understand. And Da would have, too."

It was some time before Dathan finally looked her in the eye. There was really nothing more that he could say.

"I need to go check the dock and the boats, but with this much damage, I don't hold out much hope for either," he said. "It looks like we might be stranded here for a while. I'll try to signal someone with the light, but there isn't a scrap of this wood that isn't saturated. It will be some time before it's dry enough to build a signal fire."

When the meaning of his words finally penetrated her stupor, Adrella quickly got to her feet.

"Surely someone will come looking for us."

"Sure. When they have the time," he told her grimly.

Adrella followed his gaze across the sound to the mainland beyond. She sucked in a shocked breath. Even from this distance it was clear to see that the coast had had problems of its own.

"Oh, my!"

Dathan merely nodded. "Come on. Let's get back to the light tower before it gets too dark to see." He slapped his neck, grinning wryly. "Well, the mosquitoes are back."

They moved quickly to outpace the voracious insects, but still they were covered with welts by the time they made the cover of the lighthouse. It took everything Adrella had within her to make herself enter that dark chamber again.

They slogged their way through the mud that had been left behind on the tower floor, finding a perch higher up on the spiral staircase. Dathan dug through the diminishing bag of supplies to get them something to eat. Handing Adrella an apple, he pulled one from the sack for himself.

"Tomorrow I'll see if we can't get some game or fish."

Adrella polished the apple on her sleeve, her mind not fully on what she was doing. "How will you cook it? You said there's not enough wood for a fire."

"I didn't say there wasn't enough for a fire. I said there wasn't enough for a *signal* fire. I have enough crates and such stored around here to get us a fairly good fire going, but I doubt if they will see it on the mainland."

He dropped down beside her on the stairs, his gaze wandering over her face. His attention made her nervous.

"I know how much you hate being cramped inside the tower," he told her softly. "If you prefer, we can leave the door open."

Slapping a mosquito away from her face, she grinned wryly. "And get eaten up by mosquitoes? I think not."

He shrugged. "They'll come in anyway through the

window, but maybe you're right." He rubbed a finger gently over the welts forming on her face. "They sure do seem to have taken a liking to you."

Feeling her skin tingle beneath his touch, Adrella sucked in a sharp breath and moved quickly away from him. It suddenly occurred to her how she must look, her hair hanging in a straggly mass down her back, her face covered with red welts. She winced inwardly. Even her new clothes were stained beyond repair, and her body odor after having lived five days in the same outfit suddenly made her want to scrub every inch of herself.

"What do we do now, Dathan? How long do you think it will be before someone comes to see about us?"

When she glanced at him, he looked quickly away. He pulled a canteen from the sack and handed it to her.

"I don't know," he told her. "I think it depends on how soon your father is missed. Since I have no idea how extensive the damage is in Apalachicola, I'm not certain what to expect. Eventually someone from the Lighthouse Board will come, but that could be some time."

"And what about us?" Her cracking voice spoke of her agitation.

This time he looked at her. His stormy gray eyes were filled with an intensity she had never seen before.

"We'll survive," he told her inflexibly. Rising to his feet, he moved quickly up the stairs to care for the light, effectively ending any further conversation.

The next morning Adrella awakened to azure blue skies and the sudden surety that God was in His heaven and all was right with the world. A soft breeze blew against her face when she finally stepped out of the tower to the drying sand.

The scattered debris that covered the island, however,

reminded her that things were not as peaceful as they might seem.

Dathan was nowhere in sight and Adrella felt a brief moment of panic. So much for her earlier thoughts about God's surety in caring for them. Berating herself for her cowardice, she strolled down to the water's edge and stared off toward the mainland. How long would it be before someone would come?

The gulf looked tranquil today. If not for the effects of the storm around her, one would never have thought there had been a hurricane here on this peaceful little island. Already the birds had returned and were scavenging among the waves.

Her Da would have loved it today. The thought brought with it the anguish she had been trying to hold back. She quickly shied away from the possibility of her father being in the water with the fish.

Something her father had once said came to her mind. As a child she had asked her father what became of those who died and were buried at sea. He had quoted from the book of Revelation. "And the sea gave up the dead." It was a calming thought.

Shaking herself out of her morbid musings, she went searching for Dathan and found him not far away gathering armloads of wood.

"What's that for? I thought you said it was too wet to make a fire?"

He glanced at her briefly before resuming his task. "Right now it is, but since it's dead wood, it's drying quickly."

Adrella hastily crossed to his side. "Here, let me help."

Dathan looked as though he were about to deny her help, but then he shrugged. "Okay, but be careful to watch for snakes."

Jerking her hand back from the tree branch she had been reaching for, Adrella gave him a somewhat suspicious glance.

"Are you joking?"

He continued to gather armloads of debris, always turning the piece with his foot before picking it up. "No, so be careful."

Adrella mimicked his style, and before long they had a substantial amount of wood stacked near the light tower. The sweat dripped in rivulets down both of their faces by the time they were finished.

Then Dathan began dragging large palm fronds that had been stripped from the towering trees by the hurricane's wind and loaded them into a pile. Adrella followed in his wake, curious about what he was doing.

"What are you doing now? Green palm fronds won't burn."

He lifted one dark eyebrow at her, but continued retrieving more fronds. "I'm going to build us a shelter for tonight. We can't continue to sleep in the tower. It's too uncomfortable. This way we'll be able to stretch out, and *hopefully* get some sleep."

Adrella was dubious. "What about the mosquitoes?"

Although the little critters were hiding in the heat of the day, Adrella knew they would be out in full force come evening.

Dathan grinned. "They don't bother *me*."

She settled an accusing glare on him. "How gallant of you," she told him sarcastically

The grin turned into a full-throated laugh. Adrella's heartbeat quickened, her eyes going wide. Never had she heard Dathan laugh. Truth be told, she had rarely even seen him smile. His dark features were lightened by his humor, and Adrella noticed for the first time just how devastatingly attractive Dathan could be.

"Don't worry, Adrella." He chuckled. "I won't let you be carried off. Not by mosquitoes, nor any other thing that resides on this island."

Adrella swallowed hard.

His laughing gaze met hers, but the laughter quickly faded as his look continued to plumb the depths of her suddenly frightened eyes. Frowning, he quickly looked over his shoulder to see what had caused her sudden trepidation.

"What is it?"

Adrella shook herself from her mental state, pushing her fanciful imaginings to the back of her mind. She had been listening to too many tales of the pirates who had frequented this area in times past.

"N-nothing. I was just wondering what other creatures I might have to contend with."

He returned his look to her face, his eyes narrowing dubiously. For a long moment neither one said anything. Finally Adrella cleared her throat nervously and gave him a tentative smile.

"What can I do to help?"

Readily accepting her change of subject, and her help, the two worked together in companionable silence, intermittently interrupted by one or the other voicing some thought aloud. The day passed quickly, and by midafternoon there were two rough shelters on the beach.

Although Adrella was rather skeptical about sleeping out in the open, she suddenly felt exhilarated by the idea. This was much like the book she had read by Daniel Defoe. She giggled at the idea of playing man Friday to Dathan's Robinson Crusoe.

Dathan dropped a load of wood in front of her shelter, jerking her out of her thoughts.

"I'm going inland to fill our canteen with water. We're out. I'll be back in a little while, but don't go into the ocean, whatever you do. There are jellyfish in these waters, and if they sting you, it won't be pleasant."

"Can't I come with you?" The thought of being alone was a daunting one. What if something happened to Dathan? What if there were wild animals on this island that even he didn't know about?

She heard him sigh. "Adrella, rein in that imagination of yours. I can read you like a book. Nothing's going to happen to me."

Remembering her earlier thoughts, Adrella's face paled. Could he really read her face so easily?

"I don't want you along," he told her, "because the fresh water is in the woods, and the woods are infested with mosquitoes."

Wrinkling her nose in distaste, Adrella settled back on the sand.

"Fine by me. I'll stay here. Is there anything I can do to help while you're gone?"

Dathan motioned with his hand. "Yes. Stack this wood in front of your shelter so that when I get back I can light it. The smoke should help keep the mosquitoes away."

Adrella was all in favor of anything that would protect her from those voracious insects. Nodding, she watched him move away and disappear into the woods.

Dathan headed into the interior of the forested island. Having lived here for the past two years, he knew where the fresh water pools were.

He had fashioned himself a walking stick from a piece of flotsam he had found washed up on the shore. Using it to carefully move the brush before him, he made his way to where a small pool had grown into a small lake with the heavy rain. Moccasins frequented this pool so he kept careful watch as he filled his canteen.

He hadn't wanted to let Adrella come with him because he intended to search farther in the interior to see if he could find any sign of Mangus's body. He knew the likelihood was minimal, but he had to at least try.

The island was over twenty miles long and the vegetation grew thicker the farther he traveled west. The westward side of the island was more protected from the violent weather that constantly inundated these parts.

Even here though, the storm had managed to wreak havoc, mostly with branches torn from the trees and scattered around.

He paused to watch a water moccasin slither through the brush, its undulating body gliding through the thick greenery with more ease than he was accomplishing. A raccoon scurried to get out of its way.

He grinned. Adrella had not been fond of the raccoon meat he had provided the day before. She'd said nothing, but he could see it in her face as she'd tried valiantly to chew the meat and swallow without making a face.

He chuckled at the memory. She was really being a good sport about all of this. The humor fled as quickly as it had come. Adrella's pain was never far from the surface. It was there in her eyes, a sadness that she tried for his sake to hide. He could empathize with her grief to a certain extent because he had loved Mangus as well, but he knew that his own grief could never touch the depth of despair Adrella was feeling at her loss.

Something in their relationship had changed subtly. Was it being confined with her the past several days that had increased his feelings of protectiveness toward her? The feeling that something was there between them, something they were both trying hard to ignore?

In reality she had been on his mind often since he had first met her. Although their contact had been minimal, she was a hard person to ignore.

He had at first noticed how she treated the customers at her father's store. She was always kind, even to him, although he doubted she liked him very much. At least not in the beginning. He would admit that he hadn't been the easiest person to get to know. No matter how rudely he had treated her, in the end her cheery disposition brought a smile to even his tough demeanor.

When she was happy her face lit up like the gulf on a bright spring morning. Her emerald eyes sparkled with a joy that came from deep within. It made her seem almost pretty. That spark had been missing lately, and it had hurt him to see the joy gone from her life.

What must she be thinking? Was she wondering how a girl on her own would make it without the father who had taught her everything she knew? He had wondered that himself, to his own detriment. His thoughts circled round and round in his head until he always wound up at the same starting place. He had promised to care for Adrella Murphy.

Funny, but he had never planned on getting married. He had not met the woman yet who had managed to change his mind on remaining single. Until now.

What kind of marriage would he have, wed to someone like Adrella? Was friendship a good enough basis for a marriage? He had seen numerous unions come to naught without it. Money, status, position—these were things that had been the basis of most of the matches he had known.

He supposed he liked Adrella well enough. Hers was definitely not the face that would launch a thousand ships, nor her fiery personality something that would inspire a poet's pen, but there was something about her that didn't easily allow her to slip your mind. Although she wasn't exactly pretty, her features were still pleasant enough.

Could he bring himself to actually marry her? He wouldn't say he was consumed by passion for her.

There was the time he had sat mesmerized as she combed her fingers through her hair and he had wondered what it would be like to do the same. The warmth he had felt as he watched her entrancing movements had left him feeling suddenly vulnerable.

Adrella's eyes at the time had suggested that maybe she was feeling the same kind of feelings. It had taken great will power to rein in the desire to lean forward and kiss her rosy lips. He could not take advantage of her vulnerability.

A rattle in the underbrush snapped his mind back to the moment at hand. Lifting the leaves with his long stick, he saw a rat scamper out from beneath and race off.

Taking a deep breath, Dathan admonished himself to keep his mind on his mission or he likely wouldn't live long enough to worry about what would happen to Adrella in the future.

He continued his search across the width of the island in a zigzag manner. When he reached the shore at the far side of the island, he still had seen nothing of a body— Mangus's or anyone else's for that matter. He was surprised that with the intensity of the storm that had just transpired someone lost at sea hadn't washed up on the shore of Cape St. George. It had happened in times past. That was another reason he hadn't wanted Adrella along.

He glanced up and noticed that the sun was already beginning to set. He hadn't much time if he was going to make it back in time to light the lamp. He would have to hurry.

Adrella sat for a long while watching as the sun began its slow descent. Gulls screeched overhead, and porpoises cavorted offshore among the rollicking waves. Time seemed to drag by.

With daylight beginning to diminish so rapidly, she began to worry in earnest. She knew it would soon be time to light the lamp in the tower, and she hadn't the vaguest idea how to go about it. Gnawing on her lower lip, she wondered if something had happened to Dathan after all. And if it did, what exactly could she do about it? She had no idea where he had gone.

Her tense muscles relaxed as she saw him moments later coming from the woods, his long strides eating up the distance between them. He headed straight for the light tower, and a short time later the light began to glow in the lamp room.

Before long Dathan joined her on the sand. He took a cup of oil and poured it over the stacked wood, and then lighted it. Even though the wood was not completely dry, the oil helped it to burn quickly until there was enough heat to add even damp wood to the fire without quenching it.

Watching the fire slowly take and then quickly light, Adrella suddenly jerked to a kneeling position, her eyes wide, her voice animated.

"I've got an idea!" she told Dathan, not realizing that she had gripped his hand in her excitement. "We can use the oil to light a signal fire!"

Dathan allowed his fingers to twine around hers. His eyes were inscrutable when they connected with hers, his voice oddly husky.

"I thought about that, but it would take too much oil. The wood is still too wet without using the oil to help it dry."

"But...but you still have two drums left in the tower."

He began stroking her wrist with his thumb. The tingling feeling that swept through her at his touch brought

her thoughts sharply into focus. Pulling her hand from his, she shied away from his mesmerizing gaze.

"I have to save that for the light," he told her. "I have no idea how soon the boat will come with more."

Adrella could hear the frustration in his voice.

"Frankly," he continued, "I don't have much idea about anything right now."

It suddenly occurred to Adrella that Dathan had a large responsibility resting on his shoulders. It also occurred to her that of all the men she knew, she was glad it was Dathan that was here on this island with her right now. She knew she could trust him, but the question was, could she trust herself?

"Dathan," she said quietly. "I haven't thanked you yet."

She heard him snort. "For what? Getting you trapped on an island during a hurricane? For losing your…your father?"

Adrella's mouth dropped open. She'd had no idea that he was thinking such thoughts. Could he really be blaming himself?

"It's not your fault," she told him, her voice brooking no argument.

He sat, arms curled round his upraised legs, his whole body exuding the reproach he had heaped upon himself.

"You wanted to make for shore. I should have done so."

Adrella was already shaking her head. "No. You were right. We wouldn't have made it, and then we all would have died. Da…" The little catch in her throat stopped her momentarily. "Da wouldn't have wanted that." She finished with a rush.

She could tell he wasn't convinced. "It's not your fault, Dathan Adams!" she declared vehemently, once again gripping his fingers with her own.

The warmth from his fingers seemed to flow all the

way through her body. She wanted nothing more right now than to throw herself into his arms and find the comfort she had felt once before.

Dathan cocked his head slightly, one eyebrow winging upwards. His look rested on their coupled hands briefly before a smile spread slowly across his face. Seeing his look, and remembering his comment about reading her like a book, Adrella dropped his hand as though it were a hot potato.

"I'm telling you, it wasn't your fault," she reiterated, her voice softening.

Adrella's eyes were glitteringly alive with her emotions, her flushed face very becoming in the soft firelight. How was it that the more he was around her, the more his estimation of her looks was evolving? Seeing her now, he wondered why he had ever considered her plain in the first place. She was certainly no great beauty, but she was definitely growing on him.

"Your Irish is showing," he told her with a rueful smile, his own eyes darkened by the descending night.

Dathan noticed her twitching lips. For the time being she was so concerned about his feelings that she had forgotten her own. In a way she was incredibly like her wonderful father. Mangus was always concerned for others' feelings.

"You haven't heard anything yet," she told him, deliberately thickening her Irish brogue. "Now, I'll hear no more of this foolish talk, or I'll…" She stopped, thinking a moment, before her words spilled out quickly. "I'll get the little people after you."

Dathan realized that she was attempting to defuse an already volatile situation. Both were aware of escalating emotions surfacing between the two. At first, he had thought it his own imagination, but he knew now that he hadn't mistaken that look in Adrella's eyes earlier. She was attracted to him, and he was rapidly becoming more attracted to her.

Sitting across from her, seeing the firelight on her face, realizing how alone they were, all these things added together gave him strong primeval urges that he had to quickly suppress. What on earth had come over him lately? He wasn't a man to be ruled by emotions. Forcing his gaze back to the fire, he told her harshly, "Go to bed, Adrella."

When he looked back, she had already disappeared inside her shelter.

Chapter 5

For the next week, Adrella saw very little of Dathan. He seemed to be avoiding her, and in one sense she was relieved, in another she was annoyed. She didn't understand this growing awareness between them, but Dathan didn't need to worry that she was about to throw herself at him, either.

He left early each morning and didn't return until late in the evening, in time to bring Adrella whatever means of sustenance he had procured. Usually it was fish that he caught using an old fishing pole and net he had kept stored in the lighthouse. Thankfully he hadn't brought back any more raccoons.

Today Dathan had promised that he would take her inland and show her a fresh water pool that he had found. Although he refused to allow her to bathe in it, he did promise to take a bucket and bring back enough water for Adrella to at least sponge bathe. Adrella could hardly wait.

She watched him coming across the sand toward her and felt her heart give that funny little flip flop. If she had thought that he looked like a pirate before, he certainly fit the picture now.

After nearly two weeks, the growth on his chin was more beard than whiskers. His pants clung wetly to his powerful thighs, his shirt doing the same to his muscular chest and arms. The warm copper color of his skin told its own tale of how he spent his time. Obviously he had been working on the dock again. Although the structure had been badly damaged in the storm, because it was on the side of the island that received less force from winds, it still remained partially intact. Even from this distance Adrella could see the gleam in his eyes that spoke of his vitality. Whereas she felt like a bedraggled cat, Dathan seemed to relish their situation and the obstacles he had to overcome.

He drew up in front of her, his gray-eyed scrutiny running over her briefly.

"Ready?"

Adrella nodded and got to her feet. Dathan told her to stay close behind him, and watch where she walked.

"I've seen several water moccasins around the marshes and pools," he told her.

Biting her bottom lip, Adrella said nothing as she followed in his wake. His voice had been clipped and cold, and his very posture spoke eloquently of his desire to be free from her company.

She stared at the uncompromising set of his back, aware of the tension between them.

"Have I upset you, Dathan?" she ventured softly.

He glanced over his shoulder. "What?" One eyebrow curled upward in interrogation. "What makes you say that?"

"I don't know. You seem angry for some reason."

"I'm not angry," he assured her, continuing forward. "I just have a lot on my mind."

Adrella supposed that was certainly possible. She knew she definitely did.

"I'm sure someone will come looking for us soon," she told him, not at all sure of any such thing. His only reply was a noncommittal grunt. Since it was obvious that he had no desire to talk, she dropped into silence.

When they reached the pool, Dathan carefully searched the area before nodding with satisfaction and motioning Adrella forward. She stepped gingerly over decaying logs, her long dress rustling the grass around her feet.

Wishing that she could take off her clothes and dive into the water, she settled for hesitantly lifting a handful of water and rubbing it over her face. She soon forgot to be afraid as the refreshing water cooled her flushed skin.

Dathan observed her playful antics while he filled the bucket with water, a small smile tugging at his lips. Watching Adrella play in the water like a child had caused a sudden swell of tenderness to engulf him. Her innocence touched a protective chord deep inside him that was at odds with the growing feelings of desire he had whenever he was close to her. More and more he was beginning to see her as the woman she was, and not the child he had always supposed her to be.

He supposed that the love and respect he had felt for her father had kept him from noticing such things before. Now he found himself at war with his own personal feelings and desires. Because of his growing conflict, he kept more to himself and away from her, but it was becoming harder with each passing day. He was beginning to look for excuses to be near her. Watching her now, it suddenly occurred to him that this was not exactly a good idea.

"Don't drink," Dathan warned. "This water needs to be purified."

With a nod she acknowledged his comment. Although warm from the sunlight filtering through the trees, the small pool of water was refreshing, and Adrella lost herself in the moment, playfully scattering water droplets everywhere.

She lifted her countenance and grinned mischievously at him, intending to splatter him with water. Their eyes met and the smile left Adrella's face, and swallowing hard, she got quickly to her feet, smoothing down her dampened dress.

"I'm ready to go back now," she said, her voice shaking slightly.

Dathan heard the quaver in her voice and saw the uneasiness in her wary green eyes. Clearing his suddenly dry throat, he looked away from her.

For the past few days he had studiously avoided her, hoping to figure out what was causing these oscillating feelings inside of him. One minute he wanted to take her in his arms and kiss the living daylights out of her, but the next, he withdrew inside of himself again and pushed her away, not wanting to get too close to her.

Was the isolation beginning to affect him, or was he, in truth, beginning to see Adrella as his future wife? Was it possible that the promise he had made to Mangus was already beginning to settle down upon him with sure conviction, causing his feelings to evolve?

"Dathan?"

Her quiet voice pulled him from any further reflections. Mentally giving himself a shake, he feigned a smile, offering her his hand. Hesitantly she placed her small one within his own, and squeezing gently to reassure her, he led the way back to their camp.

The whole time they trudged back through the woods, Adrella was conscious of the warmth of his fingers entwined with hers. Even the bothersome mosquitoes didn't seem such a nuisance since her mind was wholly occupied with her thoughts. The awareness between them seemed to be growing with each passing minute. Never having had much experience with men, except her own Da, Adrella was at a loss to understand the situation.

They reached their camp, and Adrella gave a small sigh of relief. While Dathan retired to the lighthouse to affect repairs, Adrella sat down in the shade of a towering slash pine. Her thoughts churned and bobbed like the waves of the ocean.

Dathan was a very handsome man. She had always thought so, but now he seemed to fill her every waking thought. Even her own father seemed like someone from a dream world, her reality receding until it encompassed only this one point in time. Even now the picture of Dathan's intent gray eyes refused to be budged from her memory.

Making a small sound of frustration, she got to her feet and wandered down to the shore. Ambling along, she watched the waves lapping at the beach, their rhythm, along with the soft breeze and vivid blue sky, soothing her into a better frame of mind. It was a truly glorious day.

Glancing out at the water, she noticed something bobbing on the waves. Cupping her hands around her eyes to shield them from the sun, Adrella watched what looked like a small keg moving ever closer. The glare from the sun reflecting off the water made it hard to tell for certain.

Each day the gulf had brought more and more debris

washing up on their small island. At first it had been exciting, like receiving presents at Christmas, but then she had come to realize that all those pieces of flotsam represented something devastated by the hurricane's forceful winds.

As the wooden barrel drew closer, Adrella could make out the words printed on its side. Harkin's Flour Mill was emblazoned in white letters across the rounded surface, and Adrella knew that here, indeed, was a treasure.

Her mind filled with images of fry bread for supper, she hurried down to the edge of the water. Taking off her lace-up boots and lifting her skirt, she waded out to retrieve the barrel. It elusively meandered on the waves just out of her reach. Each time she thought she had it, it bobbed below the water and surfaced farther out.

The water was now reaching to her waist. Although she knew how to swim, her clothes would easily weigh her down if she got into water too deep. She began to be concerned that she very well might drown if a rogue wave caught her and pulled her out to a deeper level.

She knew that if she waited, the keg should eventually wash up on the shore, that is unless it got caught it one of the currents that moved away from the island.

Deciding that the prize was worth the risk, Adrella took another step forward.

Dathan set the bucket of whitewash on the iron stairs next to him. Standing back, he surveyed his progress. The mud and water line that had extended up the tower's wall by fifteen feet had disappeared under his steady attack.

Although he was limited on the number of repairs he could make without more supplies, he had faithfully tended to his duties as keeper of Cape St. George light. He was beginning to worry, though, over the diminishing fuel reserves. If someone didn't come soon, it was possible that the light would not shine before too many more nights had passed. Thoughts of the disaster this could invoke left him worrying his bottom lip with his teeth.

He froze into immobility at a sudden piercing scream from outside. His heart slammed against his ribs. Another scream and he sprang into action.

Dumping his brush in the bucket of whitewash, he ran from the tower, stopping when he couldn't see Adrella where he had last left her. Heart thundering in panic, his eyes quickly scanned the area, coming to rest on Adrella's floundering form thrashing in the gulf water.

"Adrella!"

Running down the sandy beach, he quickly dove into the water, his firm steady strokes bringing him rapidly to her side. Shaking the water from his face, he wrapped his arm around her from behind and began easing them toward the shore. The weight of her sodden dress and his equally sodden clothes hindered his progress.

Adrella hung limply in his hold, moaning painfully. "Oh, Dathan. It hurts. It hurts something fierce."

"Just hold on, Drell," he urged. "I've got you."

Her agonized moaning sent chills coursing through him that had nothing whatsoever to do with the temperature of the water. Weak with pain, her head lolled against his shoulder.

When Dathan's feet finally touched bottom, he pulled Adrella into his arms and waded out of the water and up the beach, their soaked clothes leaving a trail of water behind them.

Breathing hard from exertion, Dathan lay Adrella down on the sand. He quickly scanned for signs of injury but could find no visible ones. Her dress clung wetly to her body, pooling water onto the sand.

"Adrella, what happened?"

The color of her face was alarming, whiter than he had ever seen it.

She moaned, rolling her head back and forth on the sand. "My foot. It *hurts*."

Lifting her gown away from her feet and legs, Dathan checked one foot and then the other. On Adrella's left foot, little lesions were beginning to appear. Tiny pieces of jellyfish tentacles clung to her skin.

Sucking in a sharp breath, he commanded her, "Be still. Don't move your foot."

"Do something, Dathan," she groaned.

Dathan shoved away her groping hand. "I said be still. Don't move. Not an inch, do you hear me?"

Tears pooled in Adrella's eyes at his hard tone. It made him feel lower than a snake's belly, but the adrenaline and fear that had raced through him made him want to strike out at something. Too weak to do anything other than comply, Adrella nodded her head lethargically.

Dathan hurried into the lighthouse tower, returning quickly with the bucket he had used only that morning for their fresh water. Running down to the gulf, he filled the bucket with saltwater and returned quickly to Adrella's side.

Taking a small stick, he gently lifted the pieces of tentacles off her skin and dumped them onto a piece of palm leaf, the whole time murmuring words of comfort. When he finished, he then thoroughly rinsed her foot with the water, flinching when she moaned again.

His angry voice rolled over Adrella in waves, contrasting greatly with his earlier attitude. "What in the world were you doing wading in the gulf? I *told* you to stay out of the water! And for goodness's sake, why did you take off your shoes?"

"I wanted to get the flour," she muttered, and Dathan

thought for certain that she was becoming incoherent. He jerked his head up.

"Flower? You risked your life for a stupid flower?" he asked sharply.

Adrella flapped her hand weakly in the direction of the beach. "No, no. Not a *flower*. There's a keg of flour. I knew we could use it."

Dathan's eyes grew wide, his look searching the beach. He noticed the keg thumping gently against the shore. Getting quickly to his feet, he ran to retrieve it. Returning to where Adrella lay, he smiled.

"Thank God," he murmured, dropping the keg beside her.

Adrella's mouth turned down in a slight pout.

"Well, now you can have some bread," she rasped, the hurt evident in her voice.

Dathan grinned, realizing that she had misunderstood his excitement over the flour. "That's the least of my worries. It's amazing, though, how God has provided for our needs."

Getting up, Dathan disappeared once again into the light tower only to return moments later with a bottle of wine that had floated up onto the shore days ago. Adrella had been all for pouring it out on the sand, but Dathan had negated that idea. One never knew when it might come in handy, and that time was now.

Adrella's eyes rounded. "I'm not drinking *that*," she told him inflexibly. "I can put up with the pain without use of artificial stimulants."

Her da had drummed into her head the evils of alcoholic beverages having at one time succumbed to their siren song himself. He hadn't whitewashed the telling, either. To think that her gentle, loving father could act like such a monster was hard for her mind to take in. She glanced fearfully at Dathan. Was he then a drinking man?

Dathan shook his head, one corner of his mouth twitching slightly. "It's not for drinking, Drell," he told her, oblivious to the fact that he had started using her father's pet name for her.

Dumping the saltwater from the bucket, Dathan then poured half the bottle of wine into it. Helping Adrella to a sitting position, he lifted her foot and gently placed it into the bucket.

The cool liquid slid over her stinging foot, and she breathed a soft sigh.

"That feels better already," she told him. Although her foot was already swelling, and the pain would undoubtedly be almost unbearable, the alcohol of the wine would stop the stinging of the jellyfish's nematocysts.

"We need to soak it for at least a half hour," Dathan told her.

When his gaze met hers, he found her green eyes sparkling with unshed tears. He felt himself melt at her obvious pain, and her evident desire to hide it. Why did the woman always feel compelled to conceal her feelings from him, especially when she was hurting? More than likely because he hadn't exactly been the most considerate of men.

Cupping her cheek in his calloused palm, he suggested in a tolerant tone, "I'm sorry I yelled. It's okay to cry, Adrella. I know it must be extremely painful."

She sniffed slightly, and Dathan wasn't certain if it was from the unshed tears, or the beginning reaction from being envenomated by the jellyfish. Watery eyes and a runny nose were only two of the usual signs of being stung.

"What's the wine for?" she finally asked, pulling away from his touch.

Sitting back, his face cleared of all emotion at her rejection of his touch. "The wine will inactivate the stingers. After a half hour I'll be able to dust your foot with the flour and scrape them off without them injuring you further."

Adrella's mouth parted slightly at her sudden understanding. "*That's* why you were so thankful for the flour."

He nodded, getting to his feet. He studied her face carefully. There was as yet no sign of a serious reaction to the venom.

"How are you feeling?"

She wrinkled her face. "My head aches, my foot is throbbing, and I feel quite nauseated." She grinned halfheartedly. "Other than that, I'm fine."

Dathan was satisfied for the moment. It was entirely possible that more serious complications could arise, but for the time being God had certainly taken care of them. Dathan was more convinced of this than ever.

"I'll be back shortly," he told her. "Don't take your foot out of the wine."

"Don't worry. I won't."

Adrella's gaze followed him as he crossed to the lighthouse and disappeared inside. She lay back on the sand, careful to keep her foot in the bucket. Closing her eyes against the sun, she tried to ignore her pounding head and the even more intense pain in her foot.

Her thoughts inevitably turned to Dathan. How could a man be so gentle one minute, and as cold as ice the next? When treating her wounds, he was all gentleness and careful concern. He would be a wonderful doctor. She wondered again what had happened to make him turn his back on medicine. What had happened to him during the war that would make him deny his Hippocratic oath?

She wanted so much to talk with him, but he always closed up like a clam whenever she tried. Often she would look over at him to speak and find him staring off into the distance, his face dark and unreadable. She hadn't the courage to face him at such junctures.

Several times in the middle of the night, she would awaken to hear him thrashing about in his shelter while he slept. She could hear him mumbling in his sleep, but from the distance of her own shelter, she could not make out any words.

When he returned after a while, Adrella kept her eyes closed, listening as he dropped to the sand beside her.

Lifting her foot from the bucket, he allowed it to dry before opening the keg of flour and dusting the affected area. He used his pocket knife to gently scrape away any nematocysts that still remained.

Rinsing off the remaining powder, Dathan then dumped the wine on the sand and poured the other half of the bottle into the bucket.

"We'll soak it one more time," he told her roughly, causing her lids to fly open in surprise at his surly tone. She searched his face, but found no emotion lurking there.

He left her again and didn't return for some time. When he did, he finished his ministrations abruptly, and then prepared their fire for the night. He disappeared once more into the tower, and before long Adrella could see the light begin its nightly vigil.

Chapter 6

Dathan lay on his back staring up at the shimmering stars above him. Feeling the need for the fresh sea air, he had chosen to forego the palm shelter where he normally slept. Hands folded behind his head, he ignored the whining insects hovering around him and contemplated the events of the afternoon. Pictures of a frightened Adrella floundering in the water started his heart beating rapidly. If he closed his eyes, he could still see the wild terror on her face. Shifting to his side, he tried to push away the feelings that held him in their grip.

This had been a day of up and down emotions for him. He felt exhausted, but his mind wouldn't let him sleep. Treating Adrella had caused painful, and conversely happy, memories to surface; memories that he had kept firmly buried deep in his mind. As though a dam had suddenly burst, images floated through his thoughts in rapid succession; a young child smiling through her tears at him after he set her broken arm, a woman cuddling her new-born infant after he had tried a risky procedure to save both of their lives, and more recently, the soldiers on the battlefield as he helplessly watched them die.

Groaning, he sat up and plunged his hands through his hair, burying his eyes beneath his palms. "No, Lord," he pleaded softly. "I don't want to remember. Please!"

He didn't want to feel again the need to help people. He didn't want to have to face the world again where there was a constant daily battle against evil. He liked his little world of isolation.

At least he had up until a couple of weeks ago. He had to admit, it was nice having someone around to talk to, and Adrella had proven to be a good companion. Comfortable. And yet, not so comfortable.

There were times when they were stranded together in the lighthouse that he had been uncomfortably drawn to her. He hadn't meant it to be, but then he hadn't intended for any of this to happen.

Perhaps the isolation was getting to him. He had heard tales of men who went insane when they were isolated from any contact with people.

Frowning, he wondered if that was why he was now having these feelings of loneliness. Why did he suddenly want to be close to Adrella, to allow her access into his steadily thawing heart? The seesaw effect of his emotions was beginning to drive him crazy.

A sudden sharp cry from Adrella's shelter brought him quickly to his feet. He was thankful there was moonlight to help him see. He pulled back the palm fronds that were used to protect her from biting insects, and saw Adrella thrashing around on the sand, her hands massaging her left leg. He ducked inside.

"What is it?" he demanded roughly, kneeling beside her and pushing her hands aside.

"My leg. Ow!"

Wrapping one large hand around her calf, he could feel the tightening muscle beneath his fingers. "Muscle spasms," he told her grimly. "They happen sometimes from the jellyfish venom. Hold on. Let me see what I can do."

Taking her leg between his two calloused palms, he began to vigorously massage the muscles. Adrella lay back, teeth clenching at the excruciating pain.

Over and over Dathan moved his hands up and down her leg until eventually the pain began to subside as the muscles relaxed. Adrella's fingers slowly unclenched as the pain began to lessen.

"Thank you," she breathed out finally, her body slowly relaxing. "It feels somewhat better now."

Dathan sat back on his haunches and studied her. "Are you sure?"

She nodded, refusing to meet his suddenly attentive gaze. She flexed her leg slightly, and he was satisfied that the spasms had ceased.

"I'm sorry I don't have anything to give you for the pain, but my medical supplies were in the keeper's cottage."

"That's okay." She sat up, placing a hand on his arm. Her eyes were dark and luminous, even in the dim light of the moon. "I've appreciated all that you've done, Dathan."

He didn't know what to say to that. How to react. Warmth traveled up his arm and wrapped itself around his mind. The awareness between them was there again, growing.

The silence grew lengthier until Dathan nervously cleared his throat. He knew he should leave, but he was suddenly reluctant to do so. He could barely see her features in the moonlight shining in through the opening, but it was enough to make him pause at what he could read in her eyes. The tension heightened between them with each passing second.

His look fastened on her lips so close to his own. He bent toward her slowly, giving her time enough to move back if she so chose. When she didn't retreat, he closed the distance, his lips moving across hers in a kiss that left him breathless.

Dathan drew back first, setting Adrella away from him. He could feel the pulse throbbing wildly in his throat. The firelight reflected in Adrella's darkened eyes, and he knew that she had been as affected as he.

Rubbing a hand behind his neck, he couldn't look her in the eye. What on earth had possessed him to do such a thing.

"I'm sorry," he muttered thickly. "I shouldn't have done that."

His apology was met with silence, and looking back at her, he found her turned away from him. Was that a tear he saw rolling down her cheek? He suddenly felt lower than a mocassin's belly.

"Good night, Adrella," he told her, his husky voice telling him more than anything that it was time to beat a hasty retreat.

Adrella nodded, refusing to speak. Lying back on the sand, she watched him as he lifted the palm fronds back into place and left the shelter.

The next morning Dathan was already absent when Adrella finally surfaced from her shelter. Pushing back the palm fronds, she blinked at the bright sunlight streaming into her eyes.

Since her stomach was queasy already, she decided to forego eating anything for breakfast. The smoked fish Dathan had left for her caused her stomach to churn even more, and she quickly turned her eyes elsewhere.

Limping across the sand, she sat down in the shade of the towering lighthouse. She leaned back against the cool white surface, letting her eyes wander across the landscape. Already the sun was shining hotly, the beautiful gray-blue gulf rippling for as far as the eye could see. Gulls wheeled and circled overhead, their screeching the only sound in the lonely world of their island habitat.

She tried to rein in her riotous thoughts, but they refused to be held in check. Dathan's kiss last night had left her shaken and confused. Her mind refused to focus on anything else. What were his feelings for her? Was he attracted to her because she was the only woman in the vicinity? Although she had heard enough stories about men and their appetites to wonder what might happen if something wasn't done soon, if the truth were told, she was actually more concerned about her own feelings. She had been hurt by his apology over the kiss, and she didn't quite understand why. Not knowing what else to do, she beseechingly lifted her eyes heavenward. "I don't even know what to say, Lord," she complained softly.

How long she sat there she didn't know, but she suddenly caught sight of Dathan coming quickly from the woods, a man trailing in his wake. Eyes going wide, she swiftly came to her feet, ignoring the pain shooting up her leg.

They came to a stop in front of her, and Dathan motioned to the man.

"Adrella, this is Mr. Carson, the lighthouse inspector. Thank the good Lord, he was sent to check on the lights in the vicinity. Mr. Carson, Miss Adrella Murphy."

Adrella stood gaping at him. "How…when…?"

Mr. Carson chuckled lightly. "It's a good thing Dathan

knows Morse code. His message was finally seen by someone on the mainland. Normally I wouldn't be coming for
another two weeks to bring Dathan his oil, but with the
storm, the Lighthouse Board thought it best to see how the
lights fared after the hurricane. When I arrived in Apalach,
I was told that something was wrong with the light. I came
as quickly as I could."

"And it's a good thing he did," Dathan remarked, his
eyes refusing to meet Adrella's. "We were almost out of
oil."

Oil? He was worried about oil? After last night oil was
the last thing on Adrella's mind.

The tension emanating from Dathan was palpable, causing Mr. Carson to frown, his look passing from one to the
other. Adrella laid a hand on his arm, drawing his attention back to her. "And Apalach? How did it fare?"

He closed his hand over hers, squeezing reassuringly.
Something flashed briefly through his eyes. "Miss Murphy, there will be time enough for explanations later. Right
now let us see about getting you off this island and back
to civilization."

Adrella's look swung to Dathan, but she could read
nothing in his hooded eyes. Feeling as though she were in
some sort of dream, she allowed Dathan to lift her in his
arms and carry her back through the woods to the dock
on the other side of the island. Only once did he look into
her face, and she could tell nothing from his visage. His
face reminded her of a stone statue she had once seen in
a park in New York City.

A boat was waiting at the dock with several men manning the oars. Surprise flashed across their faces when they
noticed Dathan carrying Adrella from the woods. Mr. Carson gave quick, staccato orders, and the men made ready

to cast off, the curious looks they surreptitiously threw Adrella's way making her very uncomfortable.

Dathan carefully set Adrella in the boat, his eyes meeting hers as his arms slid slowly away. "I'll be coming across later. I'll talk to you then."

"But…"

He shook his head. "No, I can't come now. Mr. Carson and I have to inspect the light, and I have to move those oil drums up to the tower."

For the first time Adrella noticed the barrels sitting next to the hastily repaired dock. She could do nothing but watch as the boat moved farther away from the island. Watching Dathan become nothing more than a speck in the distance, Adrella suddenly felt an overwhelming sense of loss.

As the distance increased, a feeling of numbness began creeping into her mind. The feeling stayed with her even when they landed at the dock at Apalach and Adrella was met with the knowledge of the hurricane's devastating effects.

The normally busy harbor was eerily quiet. Instead of tall-masted ships crowding the docks, all that remained were pieces of mastheads peering from the bottom of the gulf. Shattered planks from boats torn apart by the strong winds floated everywhere in the water.

Very little of the town remained. In her own isolated island world, she had almost forgotten for a time that there *was* a hurricane. Here the knowledge was obvious. The town had flooded inland from the Apalachicola River and the strong storm surge. Mud covered the once pristine streets and much of the land.

One of the men helped her onto the dock, and Adrella saw that the planking under her feet was brand new. Obviously the old dock hadn't fared well in the storm, either.

She limpingly made her way down the street, watching the people of Apalach picking up after the remnants of the storm. The whole town seemed to be milling around, trying to put things back to rights. They stared at her in surprise, but other than a quick nod or hello, they paid her little attention, each intent on picking up the pieces of their own life.

The devastation was massive. Everywhere she looked houses and businesses had been leveled. After two weeks much of the cleanup had been accomplished in the streets, but there was obviously much left to do.

She passed people who still looked dazed, like the life had suddenly left them. Others were picking through the rubble of their homes trying to salvage what they could.

A sudden sense of dread made Adrella move faster, anxious to see how her own home had fared.

When she reached the street where her father's store stood, she stopped suddenly, her heart in her mouth. The building was damaged beyond repair. The inventory had been scattered around the area, and what hadn't been drenched by rain and muddy floodwaters had been picked through by the people of the town.

She slowly made her way through the rubble, the pain at the loss of her father intensifying. What was she to do now? She had nothing!

For a time she did as others were doing and picked through the debris trying to find things she could possibly salvage. Something would have to be done about clothing because she wasn't about to stay in this dress another day.

She picked up a sodden quilt and shook it out. She recognized the pattern as the one that had been on her Da's bed, the last quilt her mother had made before she had died. It, too, was filthy with mud. Was it possible to clean it? She had to at least try. Rolling it into a ball, she set it aside.

Leaving the store portion, she moved into the area that had been her home. It took her some time to remove shattered wood from the ceilings and walls that had buried so much of their belongings. She worked tenaciously, a growing pile of debris accumulating at the side of what had once been their store.

In amongst all the rubble she was able to find little things that had at one time been taken for granted and now seemed like the most priceless of treasures.

Da's favorite cup was in the mud next to an old chair that had been ruined by the rain. The green cup had traveled with him all the way from Ireland. How many times had they sat together near a roaring fire and talked of so many things while sipping a hot cup of tea? How many times had she fixed his tea, one dash of cream and two spoons of sugar in that cup? A lump formed in her throat, tears not far from the surface.

In her bedroom she found a metal chest beneath the damaged bed just where she had left it. That it hadn't been taken was a miracle in itself, probably because it too had been buried beneath inches of mud. She took the time to thank God for leaving her something that meant so much to her. Her most precious memories were in that box, including an old picture of her mother. She unburied the treasure, wiping the mud from it with shaking fingers. She hadn't the heart to open it now in case water had gotten into it. Facing more heartbreak didn't bear thinking about right now. It went onto the small pile along with the other things she had collected.

Adrella found her father's old desk buried beneath some loose timbers. It had remained untouched except for the scarring on its wood surface and the damage done from exposure to the elements. So many times as a little girl had she sat at her father's feet by this desk while he'd managed the accounts.

The key for it was on a chain around her neck. Her father had put it there with the admonition to never remove it. She had no idea what was in the desk, but for her father to have been so adamant about it, there must be something precious.

Removing the key from around her neck, she opened the top drawer that would release the lock on all the drawers.

In the top drawer she found her father's inkwell and plume pen along with the account books. Amazingly the water that had managed to leak through the openings had done little damage to the book.

In this book was the history of the people who owed her father money. She glanced around at the people on the streets still trying to pick up the pieces of their lives. There was no way she could ever try to recoup the debts owed. It wasn't in her to ask something from someone who had already lost so much.

Opening the bottom right hand drawer, she found her father's money box. Her breath caught in her throat. Whatever was in here was the only thing that stood between her and destitution. She clutched it to her chest, afraid to even look.

She carefully opened the box, sucking in a sharp breath at the large stack of bills. There was a fortune here. She pulled it out to count it and noticed that they were all Confederate bills. Her heart dropped to her toes. Worthless! What did it mean that her father had kept these bills so long after the war had ended? Had he continued to accept the worthless money from the people of Apalach in order to help them out? She smiled sadly. That would be so like her father.

The few coins that were in the box were at least worth something, but they were not enough to live on.

Her father had recently added more stock to the store which accounted for the lack of federal money. That stock was now scattered around Apalach and buried beneath yards of debris.

Adrella sat down on the concrete stoop in front of what had once been their quarters. She stared silently, the numbness intensifying. What on earth was she to do now?

Chapter 7

For a long while Adrella sat on the stoop, her thoughts flitting from one thing to another. It was hard to settle her mind on anything. She had to make some kind of arrangements. It had never occurred to her that she would have nothing to come back to. Where was she to go? What was she to do? From the look of things around her, most of the people of Apalach were wondering the same thing.

Finally an elderly neighbor noticed her and picked her way through the debris.

"Adrella! Praise be to God! We thought you dead."

Adrella glanced up at her, hardly acknowledging her presence. She blinked large green eyes, but said nothing.

The old woman sat down next to her. "What about your pa? Where's he?"

Staring straight ahead, Adrella told her softly, "He's dead, Mrs. Sims."

Mrs. Sims sucked in her breath sharply. Reaching over,

she patted Adrella's hands where they clutched her soiled dress.

"I'm sorry, Adrella. This devil storm took too many lives." Her birdlike eyes studied Adrella from the top of her mussy hair to the bottom of her muddy shoes. "But I don't understand, where were you?"

Adrella explained about the storm, and the circumstances with her father. So engrossed was she in her own misery, she missed the darkening countenance of her elderly neighbor.

"You mean all this time you've stayed on St. George Island alone with Dathan Adams?"

Hearing the censure in her voice, Adrella turned to Mrs. Sims, her eyebrows lifting slightly. "I really hadn't any choice, Mrs. Sims. I could hardly swim the gulf to get back to shore."

Really? After all that had happened the old woman was concerned about propriety? Adrella could only shake her head in disbelief. Mrs. Sims had been their neighbor for some years and was well-known to be one of the town gossips. Heaven alone knew what she would make out of this difficult situation. Affronted at her audacity, Adrella fixed her with a steely-eyed glare.

The old lady mumbled something and quickly got to her feet. Avoiding eye contact, Mrs. Sims briefly told Adrella about her own plans to leave Apalach.

Though the elderly woman's voice rambled on, Adrella barely heard her. She should make plans of her own, but she just couldn't bring herself to care about anything right now. A sudden lethargy settled down upon her, and she gave up trying to think.

Mr. Carson finished his list, and nodded at Dathan. "That should just about do it." He smiled briefly, a rare occurrence for this rather taciturn man. "You've done well, Dathan. You're to be commended."

"Thanks."

"You'll be wanting to go the mainland?"

Dathan nodded. "Yes. There are things I need to attend to."

Mr. Carson lifted a brow. "You're welcome to ride back with us, but do you think you can make it back here in time to light the light?"

He would make it, one way or another. He had to make certain that Adrella was taken care of first or he would never be able to live with himself. The first order of business was seeing that she had a place to stay and funds enough to procure a good future. If she needed help in the store, there would almost certainly be someone who needed the work.

They began walking back toward the woods that led to the dock side of the island. Dathan held his impatience in check. There were things that needed to be attended to, he knew, but he was anxious to get to Adrella and talk with her.

"I'm sorry about the keeper's cottage," Mr. Carson continued. "We'll make arrangements right away to get it rebuilt. It might be difficult, though, to get the locals to help. We'll probably have to hire men from outside."

Striding along at the other man's side, Dathan shrugged, swatting the ever-present mosquitoes from his face. Right now that was the least of his worries.

"The people of Apalach are really good people. I'm sure they'll help."

Mr. Carson gave him an oblique glance. "That's as may be, but their hands are pretty full right now. The whole town of Apalach was almost literally wiped off the map."

Dathan jerked his eyes back to the inspector, his stom-

ach taking a sudden dive. That certainly changed things.
Did that include Mangus's store? If so he would have to
help Adrella find some kind of situation until he could
think of a way to court her. He had every intention of ful-
filling the vow he had made to Mangus, but he also knew
he would have to give Adrella time to consider the propo-
sition he intended to make to her.

"The whole town?" he asked sharply.

Mr. Carson nodded. "Pretty much so, except for those
buildings that were made of brick or had some form of nat-
ural protection. But the people are determined to rebuild.
Even now they are clearing the debris away and making
arrangements. For some it will be impossible, though."

More anxious than ever to reach Adrella, Dathan hurried his steps.

Adrella never knew when Mrs. Sims left. She sat stupe-
fied, not even noticing the movement around her. She was
unaware of Mrs. Sims across the street from her talking
with some other ladies of the town. She was also unaware
of the disapproving frowns thrown her way.

How long she sat there she had no idea, but she was
suddenly conscious of long legs standing before her eyes
totally blocking her view. She lifted tired, sad eyes and
saw Dathan, his own gray eyes full of compassion. She
clutched the money box tighter to her chest.

"Drell, I'm so sorry."

His velvet voice had the effect of breaking her stupor,
and with a cry she came upward, throwing herself into his
arms. She buried her face in his chest and allowed all the
grief to wash over her in waves, her salty tears adding to
Dathan's already damp shirt.

Taken unaware, Dathan wrapped his arms around her
and held her close. He massaged his fingers through her

scalp, holding her face against his shoulder. There was such tenderness in the way he held her that Adrella responded by crying even harder.

"It's okay, Drell," Dathan muttered. "It will be okay."

Adrella lifted a tear-swollen face to his.

"How can it be okay, Dathan? *How?* I have nothing left!"

His brooding gaze wandered over her. She must look like a bedraggled urchin standing here in tatters. Embarrassed, she tried to pull away but he wouldn't let her.

He looked around at what had once been her home and his lips compressed into a tight line. Looking down at her, he gently pushed her straggling damp hair behind her ear. "We'll think of something."

We. She loved the sound of that. She wasn't alone in this. Dathan was here to help. Whereas before she would never have given him a second thought for help, their friendship had grown to a point that she could no longer imagine her life without him.

"We'll think of something," he reiterated, his voice not more than a whisper.

He once again wrapped her in his arms and the tears that had almost ceased commenced once again in a torrent of misery.

Adrella finally noticed some women across the street watching them, their expressions full of outrage. Wondering about their odd behavior, she mentally shrugged and concentrated on the comfort she found being in Dathan's arms.

It was a long time before Adrella's tears ceased and her shaking stopped. Dathan set her away from him, his eyes searching hers.

"Drell, I have to get back to the light, but we need to

talk." He glanced around him, not certain where to go, but knowing that they couldn't stay here.

He noticed some women across the street looking their way and whispering. When they observed him watching them, they hurriedly turned away. He frowned, continuing to watch them, and noticed that they surreptitiously looked his way from time to time. Probably a bunch of gossips appalled that he was holding Adrella so close. Well, let them gossip. Adrella needed his comfort right now and he wasn't about to worry about what people might think.

But then he remembered the odd little comments the oarsmen had made to him on the way to the mainland. One of the oarsmen had made a lewd comment about being stranded on an island with a woman, but his mind had been elsewhere and he had paid it no heed. The others had responded with crude laughter. He had made some biting comment to them and they had settled into silence. Things were beginning to make more sense now.

"Where will you stay?" he asked absently, his eyes searching the area around them, noting that several others had stopped to stare at them. He shifted uneasily under their regard.

Adrella shrugged apathetically.

From the looks on people's faces, Dathan realized the conjectures people were making. For his own part he could handle the tittle tattle, but he refused to allow Adrella to suffer for something she'd had no control over. His chin settled into firm lines. "Come with me."

Adrella took his hand. She was clutching a metal box that he recognized as Mangus's money tin. He said nothing about it, merely offering to carry it for her. She handed it over without comment.

They walked down the street noticing the number of people scrounging through the debris. Apalach was a small enough town that most people knew everyone, or at least almost everyone, in town.

Dathan, on the other hand, knew hardly anyone. For an instant he felt ashamed that he hadn't taken the time to get to know more people. Sure, he was isolated on the island, but he crossed to the mainland often to send mail to his family in New York and pick up supplies from the store.

They passed a young woman kneeling in the middle of what had once been a small cottage but was now little more than a shell. She clutched something in her hand and was softly sobbing, rocking back and forth. Adrella noticed her and hurried to her side, Dathan following more slowly. He had always had a hard time seeing a woman's tears.

When they got closer he could see that she was holding a wedding picture tightly against her chest. Adrella knelt beside her, taking one of the woman's hands into her own.

"Alice! Alice, what is it?"

The woman stared at them with tear-drenched eyes. "John…"

It was all she could say before she once again burst out sobbing. Her keening cry raised the hair on the back of Dathan's neck.

Adrella patted her hand comfortingly. "Is he…is he…?"

Alice nodded. "Dead. His ship was coming in from the West Indies but they were caught by the storm." There was a catch in her voice. "The ship went down with all hands."

"Oh, Alice!" Adrella wrapped her in a consoling embrace. "What can I do to help?"

Dathan stared at her in openmouthed amazement. She had lost everything, including the one person she loved most in the world, and here she was offering comfort to someone else. Perhaps it was because of that loss that she was able to do so, but he had to admire her for it. He was beginning to understand what a truly amazing woman she was.

Alice shook her head. "There's nothing to do. I'm going back home to Louisiana to live with my folks." She started sobbing again.

Adrella slowly, reluctantly rose to her feet. "Well, if you need anything, let me know."

The other woman scarcely noticed when they walked away. Dathan could almost see the thoughts going through Adrella's head. Alice had family to go to, what did she have?

They walked for some time in silence. As they were passing what had once been an alley between two buildings, they heard a soft mewling sound coming from the rubble.

"What was that?" Dathan stopped, listening.

They listened until they heard the sound again. He and Adrella searched through the rubble, turning over wood and other items that had been blown here by the hurricane's forceful winds.

When they heard the cry again, Dathan followed it until he decided it was coming from behind a stack of splintered planks. Pulling them aside, he found a small kitten. Huddled and fearful, it made a pathetic sight.

"Oh!" Adrella pushed by him, lifting the sodden kitten into her arms, ignoring the further soiling of her dress. "Oh, you poor thing."

It was hard to tell the kitten's color it was so covered in mud. Adrella wiped as much of the mud off as she could, revealing what appeared to be white fur except for one black spot surrounding one of its eyes. The kitten shivered violently, its fur saturated with muddy water that chilled as the air hit it.

"Whose do you think it is?" Adrella asked him, her tone anxious.

"There's no telling where he came from," Dathan answered, listening to see if he could hear any other movement in the pile. "It's a miracle he's still alive. He must have been able to scavenge for enough food to survive."

Adrella lifted the kitten. "She," she answered him before once again cuddling it close. "It's a she."

Dathan pushed a hand back through his hair, frowning. "So now what are we going to do about her?"

Adrella stared at him in surprise. "We'll take her with us, of course."

That's what he was afraid of. "Adrella…"

She looked up at him, eyes glistening with unshed tears. He sighed heavily. Somehow he knew how this was going to end.

"She's all alone, Dathan!"

"I'm sure we can find it a good home. We can't take it with us. *We* don't even have a home."

Her bottom lip started to tremble and Dathan closed his eyes, gritting his teeth.

"Be reasonable, Drell," he told her in exasperation. "I can't take it to the island and you have nowhere permanent to stay."

"I'll take care of her," she stated firmly.

He could see there would be no way to sway her. The kitten was a way to replace something she had loved and lost. He knew it as certainly as he knew that his name was Dathan Adams.

She looked up at him hopefully. He sighed again.

"So," he yielded. "What are you going to name her?"

Her eyes went from tearful to glowing in an instant. The first smile he had seen since he'd arrived in Apalach made him glad he had capitulated.

Adrella hugged the kitten close. "Grace. I'm going to call her Grace. It's only by God's grace that she was spared."

Dathan picked up Adrella's money box. Somehow he just knew this wasn't a good idea but it didn't look like he had much of a choice. Taking her by the arm he started down the littered street.

"Fine. Now let's see if we can find you a place to stay." He looked from her to the kitten. "One that will take cats."

He took her to the church, but there were already an enormous number of people lodging within its walls. Built of brick, it was one of the few buildings that had managed to weather the storm.

"I'm sorry," the minister told them, his tired eyes sympathetic. "There's really no room."

People were in every chamber, more people than he would have thought the building could hold at one time. Still, where else did the people have to go?

"Is there nowhere you could put Adrella up?"

The minister looked harassed. "I'm sorry. I wish we could house more, but there just isn't room. Every house that survived this monster storm has more people than it can comfortably fit. Any more and conditions could become dangerous."

Dathan's next words jerked Adrella's attention to him.

"Will you marry us then, Mr. Evans?"

Adrella was limping up and down in the parlor of the church, her green eyes flashing with anger when Dathan entered the room. Her flushed face warned of an impending storm and she saw him stiffen in preparation for the battle to come.

"You're loonier than the gulf!" she expostulated. "Have you gone daft?"

"I promised your dad…" he began, but she ruthlessly interrupted him.

"Oh did you, now," she fairly purred, her Irish brogue intensifying. "Well, and isn't it a good thing that I'm not me da! Now you won't have to keep your promise."

Dathan moved toward her warily.

"I have every intention of keeping my promise," he told her inflexibly.

Adrella stood feet apart, fists braced on her hips. Fiery green eyes glared into cold gray ones. A warning flashed through her eyes that Dathan chose to ignore.

"What are your alternatives?" he asked, his voice dangerously low.

Stumped for an answer, Adrella merely glared at him.

He took her by the shoulders, but she slapped his hands away. "I'll walk the streets first," she hissed between gritted teeth. Regretting the words the instant they'd left her mouth, she glanced at Dathan, intent on recanting her statement.

The savage look on his face took much of the ire from Adrella. She took a hasty step backward in retreat, but she was too late. Dathan jerked her forward, his fingers biting into the flesh of her upper arms. She glared impotently into his outraged face.

"Over my dead body," he ground out ferociously. "Don't ever let me hear such nonsense again!"

Adrella gave a few seconds thought to fighting him, but never having seen Dathan in such a black mood, she prudently decided not to.

"You don't *need* me," she told him stonily, and allowed her body to slowly relax against him as the anger faded only to be replaced by hurt. The tautening of his features assured her that he hadn't missed the pain in her voice.

"It's not a matter of what *I* need."

Loosening his hold slightly, he pushed a lock of hair behind her ear. The brief contact made her shiver.

"Don't you see, Adrella? You need me, and I'm beginning to see that I need someone as well. Someone who will keep me from turning into a crotchety old hermit." He stared hard into her eyes. "We would be good together."

Adrella watched the emotions chase across his features. He had said nothing about love, but looking into his face, she came to the startling conclusion that she really *did* want to be this man's wife. Although he hadn't said he was in love with her, *she* was in love with him! That was why she felt so unsettled around him, why she felt her heart give that odd little jump whenever he was near, why he was forever in her thoughts. It all made sense now! Following this thought, another one brought her head up sharply. Had Da known even before she had? Was that why he had arranged a match between them? And if he had surmised Adrella's feelings, was it possible that he had seen something in Dathan, also? Was it possible that he might care for her, and not even know it himself?

"Adrella, think about it. Yours isn't the only reputation to consider here."

She stared at him in surprise. "What do you mean?"

"There's not a man in this town that wouldn't tar and feather me if I didn't do right by you. And I wouldn't blame them one bit. I would feel the same. They knew and loved your dad, they know and love you. They don't really know anything about me."

The door opened behind them, and Mr. Evans cleared his throat uneasily. He must have thought her a raving Banshee the way she had railed at Dathan. He had offered the parlor for them to air their differences and Dathan had forced her into the room, firmly shutting the door behind him until he could speak to the minister alone and give her time to think.

Well, she had had time to think, all right. Time to realize that she had foolishly fallen in love with a man she barely knew and who, until two weeks ago, had scarcely given her the time of day.

Dathan had said they would be good together. What exactly did that mean? Was he tired of being alone? More to the point, was it true what he'd said? Would his reputation be tarnished if she didn't agree to marry him? She couldn't take that chance with someone else's life.

"Has Miss Murphy decided?" Mr. Evans asked hesitantly.

Dathan slowly released Adrella, one dark eyebrow winging upward in question. His eyes never left hers.

Adrella swallowed hard. "Yes, Mr. Evans," she replied softly. "The answer is yes."

Chapter 8

Adrella stood beside Dathan in her borrowed wedding finery. The dress was one Mrs. Evans had lent her after helping Adrella wash the grime from her tired body. The soft blue color did nothing for her complexion, her white face almost as pale as the material. It hung loosely on her petite frame, Mrs. Evans being a much more robust lady. Still, she wouldn't complain. Anything was better than the tattered green dress she had worn for two weeks now. If she never saw a green dress again, it would be too soon.

She was grateful to the minister's wife for arranging a hot bath for her, allowing her a few minutes to settle her turbulent feelings. The bath and clean garments had refreshed her body, but her mind was still dull with fatigue and sorrow.

What was she doing? Like any girl, she had dreamed about what her wedding would be like. After a few years, she had really given up hope, but the dreams were still there. They had always included a bridegroom standing beside her, smiling at her with love in his eyes. Not a taciturn man, mouth pressed tightly together as though to hold back the words he was expected to express.

Dathan might not have been the smiling groom she envisioned in her dreams, but he was everything else she could have wished for. He had changed into clean clothes that Mr. Evans had procured for him somewhere, and he had taken the time to shave. Could a man be more breathtaking?

Several of the people from Apalach who were staying in the church were here to witness her binding of herself to a man who apparently could barely stand to look at her. His grim countenance was hardly encouraging.

The whispers around them made Adrella flinch inwardly. She had known these people for most of her life. How could they believe that she and Dathan would do something improper? How could they be willing to judge her so? After all that had happened to this town, after the things her father had done for them.

"Adrella?"

Adrella started at the minister's voice. She stared at him uncomprehendingly. He coughed slightly.

"I said, do you take this man to be your lawfully wedded husband?"

She glanced at Dathan's set face, his eyes dark and unreadable. If only he would give some indication that he had some kind of feeling for her besides a chivalrous desire to protect her from gossip. She hesitated a moment too long and Dathan lifted a persuasive eyebrow.

"I...I do."

He asked the same of Dathan and Dathan's voice answered him loud and clear, unlike her own soft, stuttering reply.

Mr. Evans glanced from one to the other. "Do you have a ring?"

Adrella did. Her father's ring. A ring that signified a loving commitment between two people who adored each other. How could she do this? Her father meant for that ring to go to the man she married, a man who would love her as her Da had her mother. There was over twenty years of love bound up in that gold band. She opened her mouth not knowing what she was about to say but was startled into silence by Dathan's voice answering instead.

"We do."

She stared at him in surprise, but before she could think of what to say, the minister continued with the service. The whole ceremony had become surreal. Somewhere along the line she had lost control of the whole situation. But then, had she ever been in control? From the time she had stepped into her father's skiff until today, her life had taken an unexpected turn. Dathan's voice was like an echo in a dream, seeming to come from far away.

"With this ring, I thee wed."

He took her hand and slid on a delicate ring of sapphires encrusted with diamonds. Her jaw dropped in surprise. Where had he gotten such a beautiful ring? The twinkling of the gems in the soft candlelight was mesmerizing.

"Adrella?"

She blinked at Mr. Evans in confusion.

"Your ring," he prompted gently.

She slowly removed the chain from around her neck that held both her father's ring and the key to her father's desk. She had placed the ring there for safekeeping against the hope that one day she would have a husband to give it to. Now that hope was being realized, but under dismaying conditions.

She clutched the ring tightly in her hand, unable to bring herself to look at Dathan's face.

"Repeat after me," the minister intoned. "With this ring, I thee wed."

Adrella's voice quavered as she repeated the lines. Sliding the ring onto Dathan's finger, she finally looked up at him. The ring fit him perfectly. Was it perhaps a sign?

He glanced from her to the ring and for the first time he smiled and she was reassured somewhat, some of the strain sliding from her tense shoulders.

"I now pronounce you man and wife. You may kiss your bride."

Dathan's kiss was brief and, she felt sure, must have been meant to be reassuring. Instead it only gave her more questions. It was nothing like the kiss they had shared on the island. That kiss had shattered her world.

Dathan had to keep her from pitching forward as the room swam dizzily around her. What had once seemed surreal was now frighteningly concrete. Oh, what on earth had she gotten herself into?

Dathan had left Adrella with the minister's wife while he tried to make arrangements about provisions to take back to the island. Mr. Carson from the Lighthouse Board had agreed to meet him at the lumberyard to see what could be furnished in the way of supplies to rebuild the keeper's house.

In the meantime they would have to manage as best they could with what little they could find. Everyone here was in the same situation, but if you had money, money talked. And he had money . Only one more thing that needed to be discussed with his new bride.

Just the word brought him up short. He had really done it! He had married a woman he barely knew in order to fulfill a promise to a man he had greatly admired. He and Adrella were so very different it would take some maneuvering to make this work, but he was determined to try.

He felt a little guilty using guile to coerce her into marriage, but it was the only thing he could think of. He knew that she would have been willing to put up with a ruined reputation rather than marry a man she didn't love, but she couldn't bear the thought of him doing the same. At the same time, what he had said was probably more than a little bit true. He had noticed some of the men glaring at him, and while he wasn't concerned what anyone thought, he had used it to his advantage. He was thankful that they would be on the island and not here in town.

His parents would be livid. He knew that they had someone already picked out for him back in New York, someone who would grace a mansion and help further the Adams kingdom. They were just waiting for him to "come to his senses" as his father had stated it. They had been waiting for seven years. A wry smile tilted his lips. He sure hoped Evangeline wasn't still waiting as well.

Not that he had anything against Evangeline. She was everything a society wife should be: beautiful, cultured, talented. When she walked into a room draped in jewels and the most expensive clothes money could buy, all heads turned her way.

Trying to imagine Adrella in such a setting was enough to boggle the mind. Still, it gave him a sense of extreme satisfaction to have thwarted his parents' plans for his life. He and his father had never seen eye to eye on the important things of life. And unlike his parents, Adrella was a Christian in the true sense of the word.

As he made his way toward the warehouse, he noticed that the streets were becoming more deserted as the day wore on. Those who intended to stay and rebuild were headed for the night to either the church or one of the other homes and warehouses that were still standing. He picked up his pace, knowing he hadn't much time to get back to the island.

He reached the lumber mill and heard the sound of machinery busily preparing the wood that would be necessary to rebuild this small town. The lumber mill had withstood the storm well and was producing as fast as was humanly possible, but with the amount of planking necessary, it would be some time before orders were completed.

"Dathan. Over here."

Dathan turned at Mr. Carson's call. He was standing next to the mill owner and both men were watching as he crossed over to them.

"Hello, Mr. Panganopolis," Dathan called in greeting. The old Greek had been here since long before the war. He had made his fortune felling trees and producing the turpentine the area had become known for.

"Dathan."

"Mr. Panganopolis says that it might be some time before he can get the lumber for the lightkeeper's cottage," Mr. Carson told him.

Dathan looked to Mr. Panganopolis for verification. The other man nodded.

"'Fraid so, Dathan. I can only do so much at a time and I'm pretty much booked solid."

Shoving his hands into his pockets, Dathan rocked back on his heels. "How much would it take to make the keeper's cottage a priority?"

Mr. Panganopolis cleared his throat uneasily. "Well, Dathan. It's not a matter of money. People in this town need somewhere to live as well." He motioned with a hand. "You can see how it is. Folks gotta have a house, specially when they have young 'uns."

Dathan understood that well enough, but he wasn't about to have Adrella sleeping in a tent any longer than necessary. The mosquitoes were already eating her alive. She had put up with more than any woman should have to, and he was determined to take better care of her in the future. He had never used his money to work his way before, but he was about to do so now.

"How much?"

"Now see here, Dathan," Mr. Carson objected. "The department that oversees the lighthouses only has so much money allotted and more than your island was affected."

"I understand that," he agreed, still watching Mr. Panganopolis. "How much and how long?"

The other two men exchanged glances. The lumberman shrugged. "If I could hire more people, two weeks." He held up a hand as Dathan was about to speak. "But the men in this town are busy trying to rebuild their own homes."

"And I suppose these men are getting their lumber on credit?"

Mr. Panganopolis frowned. "Well, of course. It will be some time before they get their fishing businesses up and going again. It'll take time, but I have faith they will repay when they can."

Dathan was impressed with the man's genuine concern. His father wouldn't have thought twice about calling someone's debt. It was encouraging to know there were still people who had their priorities in life straight. He had to wonder if his own were.

"I'm asking again, how much?"

The fact that he was acting like his father when he wanted to get his way was extremely unsettling. He felt a little niggle of guilt that he quickly squashed. He was doing this for Adrella.

"Right now I'm trying to give the lumber at as close

to cost as I can manage. Twenty cents a foot," Mr. Panga-nopolis told him.

"I'll give you a dollar and in cash. I'll take all that wood over there to begin with."

Both men's jaws dropped at this announcement and they stared at him as though he had grown two heads.

"There is no way the department will authorize such," Mr. Carson told him angrily.

"I wasn't suggesting they do," Dathan refuted. "I will pay for it."

"You!" Both men spoke in unison.

Dathan nodded. "That's right. I will stop by the bank and make arrangements to have money wired here."

Since the bank was made of brick as well as the church, it was one of the few buildings still standing as well. He doubted, though, that the bank owner, Jasper Howard, would be allowing people to camp out in his building like the minister and others whose establishments had fared better than most. Jasper was a mean-spirited, selfish little man and it galled Dathan to have to do business with him, but he would swallow his pride ten times over if it meant a proper place for Adrella to live.

The lumberman shrugged helplessly. "It's not just about money. Other people got a right to a home as well as you."

"I agree," he told him. "At eighty cents a foot profit though, you should be able to hire more men which should make the process that much faster, and you will still make a hefty profit for yourself."

The older man rubbed his chin thoughtfully. "I suppose that's true enough. I could send a wire to Mobile and see if there's any men that need the work. Maybe some of the men in Apalach would be willing to work a half day for their own planking and that would give them a half day to build on their own homes as well."

Dathan doubted if he would have a problem finding help since so many men coming back from the war were still trying to find their way back onto their financial feet.

Mr. Carson said nothing, but his look spoke volumes. He crossed his arms, shaking his head. "And do you have that much money, Mr. Adams?" he inquired icily. "The department can hire men from outside the area, but not without funds."

"I do. Now, do we have a deal, or not?"

The two men looked at each other. Mr. Panganopolis shrugged and held out his hand. "We do. You get the money, and I'll get you the lumber."

"Done," Dathan told him.

Adrella paced the halls of the church waiting for Dathan's return. Grace was cuddled against her shoulder. The kitten's silky fur tickling her chin and her soft purring brought a slight smile to Adrella's face. In the short time she'd had the kitten she had fallen in love with her.

Mrs. Evans had allowed her to wash the kitten and had given her a clean rag to wrap it in. Its shivering was only now subsiding.

"Poor baby," Adrella whispered, cuddling it closer but taking care not to hurt its injured hindquarters. A small fragment of wood had impaled the kitten's back leg, but Dathan had removed it and bandaged the cut.

The kitten reminded her of herself, lost and hurting. But whereas the kitten's hurt was physical, hers was more mental. She had been chiding herself for the past few hours over her sudden marriage. She was still having a hard time accepting it as a reality. How then must Dathan be feeling?

Yes, she loved Dathan, but she should never have taken advantage of his sense of duty. She had talked herself into believing everything would be all right because of her own love for Dathan. She had fully convinced herself that that one soul-stirring kiss on the island had shown that he had feelings for her as well. Maybe not love, but something that could grow into it in time. His face when taking his vows told her otherwise.

He had said they needed each other, but was that really true? It had been common in Ireland for people to marry for expediency, but that was no excuse. She should have known better. Frustrated at her own circular reasoning, she flung herself down on a chair and sighed.

Had she done Dathan irreparable harm by marrying him, or would the greater harm have been in not marrying him? The thought of an annulment fled her mind as swiftly as it had come. Vows before God were sacred and not to be taken lightly. And Dathan? She had never met a man who was so duty bound.

The door opened and Dathan walked in. He gave her a brief glance before setting down a burlap bag that he had slung over his shoulder.

"I've managed to gather a few supplies, enough to last at least a week," he told her. "The rest are being loaded into a boat for our return to the island."

She wondered what was in the bag but refrained from asking. Whereas on the island they had formed a kind of bond out of need and had become friends, now there was a strain between them that was even greater than before.

He handed her the bag. "For you."

Surprised, she took the bag from him and, handing him the kitten, untied the rope holding it together. Inside she found a lovely sapphire-blue taffeta dress and matching crochet lace shawl. She drew the dress from the bag and held it up against her shoulders. She had never seen anything so lovely.

"Wherever did you get this?" she breathed.

Laughter danced in his eyes turning them more blue than gray. "Mrs. Allison's dress shop fared better than most. She was rather loquacious in her condemnation of the fact that the people of Apalach hadn't taken her advice and built their homes of brick."

Adrella had to chuckle at that. Mrs. Allison was the town busybody, always trying to run people's lives, but she had a heart of gold. Everyone loved her.

"Do you like it? It should be the right size. Mrs. Allison remembered your size from the green dress she made for you."

She glanced at the dress not knowing what to say. Surely this dress had to have cost a small fortune. It was one of Mrs. Allison's Paris designs, dresses that only the wealthy in town could afford.

The green dress she had worn to the island was one of Mrs. Allison's less expensive gowns, but equally well made and beautiful. At least she had thought so at the time. But this…

"Didn't she have anything plainer? This will hardly do for trekking around the island."

His slow smile told her that he knew exactly what she was thinking.

"Don't worry about it, Adrella. It's paid for, leave it at that and just enjoy it."

He had to be kidding. They were married now and it was up to her to make certain that they could live within their means. It was a way of life passed on to her by her father and she wasn't about to suddenly forsake it.

He took the bag from her and handed back Grace. "Get changed. We need to leave as soon as possible."

"You want me to wear this now?" she asked dubiously.

He cocked his head. "Is there a problem?"

"It's just…well…"

"Yes?"

"I don't think the seawater will do it any good."

Dathan laughed and Adrella felt that little catch in her heart again. He was such a different man when he laughed. She loved the little lines that fanned out from his eyes.

"My practical Adrella," he said, smiling. "There's more where that came from. Please. Put it on for me."

If it would cause him to smile like that again, she would be glad to do just about anything he said.

Chapter 9

Adrella sat beside Dathan in the skiff as they made their return trip to the island. Part of her was filled with dread, the other part was feeling somewhat excited at what lay ahead. Dathan hadn't been happy to have her along, but in the end, there was no way around it.

Things would be different this time, although she would still be sleeping outside and not in a house. Dathan had somehow arranged to scrounge up an old army tent, and now they wouldn't have to sleep on the sand but, instead, on blankets. Where or how he had managed this, she had no idea. It wasn't the first time he had shown his resourcefulness. She was only now beginning to realize just how intelligent and capable he was. She felt a small thrill of pride in knowing that he belonged to her.

She carried her mother's quilt on her lap. Mrs. Evans had helped her to wash it before they had to leave and it looked almost like new, although it would never be as pristine as it had been before. She hugged it close against the chill air blowing across the water.

Grace was snuggled down inside of it, her soft mewling a protest at the undulation of the rocking boat. Adrella stroked her head gently, trying to comfort her as much as possible under the circumstances. Maybe Dathan had been right and she should have left the kitten with Mrs. Evans, but she just couldn't bring herself to do it. It reminded her too much of herself. Lost and confused.

It was now the first week of November, and although the gulf was still fairly warm, the temperatures dropped quickly when combined with the fine sea spray and the approaching evening. She was thankful for the new dress and shawl Dathan had purchased for her. She would have preferred something much less elaborate, but then, as the old saying went, beggars can't be choosers.

She glanced back at her husband manning the oars. He, too, was wearing new clothes. The cable-knit gray sweater he wore matched the color of his eyes, those eyes that were staring out over the gulf, his mind obviously miles away.

"Dathan?"

He turned his attention to her. "Hmm?"

She twirled her wedding ring on her finger. The blue sapphires exactly matched the dress she was wearing, the stones shining brightly in the waning light of the sun.

"Where did you get this ring?"

He looked away from her. "It was my grandmother's. I retrieved it from the bank in Apalach."

Before or after he had asked her to marry him? Demanded was more like it. Had he planned all along to use circumstances to his benefit so that he could fulfill his promise to her father? She glanced up at him and found him watching her.

"I know what you're thinking, and no, I didn't plan this. But I'm not sorry it happened, either."

The timbre of his voice warned her that he didn't want to discuss it any further. She opened her mouth, but then snapped it shut. The hurt must have shown on her face because Dathan sighed heavily.

"Adrella, there are some things we need to discuss. I had hoped to wait until we were settled, but maybe it's best if we get them out in the open now." His eyes filled with laughter. "At least this way you won't be able to run away in a temper."

He was amused by the words. She was not.

"We need to talk about our marriage," he stated more seriously.

Adrella swallowed hard. Apprehension traced its icy fingers along her spine. Ever since she had made her hasty wedding vows, she had wondered what Dathan expected of her. That she loved him went without saying, but exactly how did he feel about her? What did he really expect from a wife he had married out of duty?

"Am I wrong in believing that we have become friends over the past two weeks?" he asked.

Adrella shook her head. "No, Dathan, you're not wrong, at least as far as I'm concerned."

"And do you trust me?"

Did she? Yes, she did. There was no doubt in her mind that everything he had done, he had done for her. If there was a slight hesitation in her nod, it wasn't due to a lack of trust. The look he threw her was skeptical, but he decided to continue.

"You already know that I am…was…a doctor." He paused and she could tell he was hesitant to go on.

"Yes?" she encouraged.

"I come from New York and my family is extremely wealthy. As am I."

The color drained from Adrella's face. That was the last thing she had expected him to say.

"I haven't told you much about my family, but my parents are both alive. My father has his fingers in several pies; he is well diversified, but the main one is steel." He hesitated, searching her face. "In actuality, as an only child, I am really an heir to an empire."

He made the statement in such a matter-of-fact tone it took Adrella a moment to fully realize what he had just said. The look on his face assured her that he was not joking. She blinked at him, her thoughts in sudden turmoil. She came from plain folk, people who farmed the land and worked hard with their hands. Her people had been slaves to the landed gentry for ages, and now Dathan was declaring that he was one of those people that she heartily despised and had fled Ireland to escape.

During the war in this country her father and she had been hard-pressed to side with the state they lived in when it came to the slavery issue. Although they loved their home, they knew what it was like to be nothing more than slaves. It was an abomination that put her on her mettle. Now what was she to say to his declaration?

"Adrella, I'm telling you this because I need to make arrangements with the bank to have some money sent down from my father. I want to be able to provide better for you..."

"I don't need your money," she interrupted quietly, her accent thickened by her stress. She would not become one of those snobbish people, no matter how much she loved Dathan.

He sighed. "I understand how you feel." He held up his hand when she would have broken in and she fumed in silence. "Your father and I talked many a time about the injustices of life. I knew how you both felt about rich people. That's why I didn't want to tell you."

Her Da would be horrified to know that Dathan was, in fact, gentry. Although in America there were no such things as lords and ladies, there might as well have been. The attitude was much the same. Had she known this about him before, she never would have married him, loving him or not.

She was filled with sudden misgivings about her future. She had no idea what it took to be a wealthy man's wife. The fact was, she had no desire to find out. She had been content when she thought they would just be two lonely people struggling together. Things were different now.

Adrella had no pretensions about herself. When they had first arrived on the shores of the States, they had landed in New York. Those first months she had learned a lot about the wealthy. Their disdain for the very people who made their lives so good was intolerable to her.

She and her Da had been looked down on by not only the wealthy, but their hired help as well. They had been made to feel like second-class citizens. She was still the same person, the same person his kind had looked down upon. And him? What kind of man was he really?

"Adrella, look at me."

She did so reluctantly. He too often could read her thoughts.

"This changes nothing between us."

Shaking her head, she told him quietly, "It changes everything. You lied. You lied about everything. Who you are, what you are."

Anger burned in his eyes. "I never lied to anyone."

She glared back at him. "Pretending to be a lighthouse

keeper? Acting like you had little money and asking me Da for credit?"

The boat slowed as he stopped rowing. He leaned forward over the oars, angry color filling his face.

"I *am* a lighthouse keeper, and proud of it! And I try to live on what I have earned on my own merit. A lightkeeper's pay is minimal and there were times when I ran low on funds. I didn't ask your father for credit. He saw I needed it and, being the man he was, he offered it to me."

"Why didn't you just ask your family?"

She realized her voice sounded rather snide, but she couldn't help it. Too often her Da had gone without because he overextended credit to others. The Confederate money was proof of that. And this man had a fortune at his disposal yet took advantage of her father's kind heart. She knew it was unreasonable to blame it all on Dathan, but she had to direct her anger and hurt somewhere and he was the closest target at hand.

When Dathan had been just a lighthouse keeper who struggled to make ends meet they'd had something in common. Now, with just a few words, they were miles apart and she was suddenly very frightened. What exactly was he trying to tell her?

He began rowing again, putting his anger into action. The boat skimmed across the water at a much faster rate. The silence between them was heavy with unsaid words.

It was some time before he finally spoke again. When he did, his voice was strangely quiet and she leaned toward him to better hear.

"My father and I didn't part on very good terms. He was opposed to my going into the army. He wanted me to stay behind and run the company with him."

It suddenly occurred to her that for the first time in their acquaintance, Dathan was finally opening up to her. How often had she tried to get him to open up about his past, yet he wouldn't. He was giving her the honor of treating her as a wife, giving her a glimpse inside his life and mind. Pushing away her feelings of inferiority and her insecurities, she tried to accept that whatever he told her was because they would be sharing their future together.

"Go on," she prompted uneasily.

His face registered his surprise at her sudden attentiveness and she knew that he hadn't meant to say what he did aloud. After a moment he continued.

"We had a big argument. He threatened to disown me if I went into the army."

"But you went anyway," she reasoned.

"Obviously. Anyway, he not only didn't disown me, he made certain that I was given a captaincy."

"You called his bluff."

His eyes glittered with feelings held in check. "I did. Since then, we have kept in minimal contact."

"I take it they don't know about me."

He met her look head on. "They will soon enough. That's what I was trying to tell you. I have to contact him to access my accounts."

Adrella felt the bottom drop out of her stomach. If his father was such a hard man, what on earth was he going to think of her? One couldn't make a silk purse out of a sow's ear no matter how beautiful the clothes.

They were nearing the dock. By mutual consent they withheld further discussion until a more appropriate time. Dathan stowed the oars and leaped from the boat, the water coming up to his knees. He pushed the boat against the dock and Adrella hurriedly climbed onto the wharf and accepted the mooring line he handed her. She tied it to the post.

Dathan grasped the dock with both hands and quickly

lifted himself from the water. Adrella couldn't help but admire his toned physique, the way his muscles rippled even under the bulky sweater he wore. He reminded her of the sea, strong and powerful at times, gentle and kind at others. Unfortunately he was just about as deep.

He climbed back into the boat and began handing Adrella the supplies he had managed to procure before they'd left, along with the few things she'd salvaged from her home. Adrella placed the kitten in a small crate that held bags of flour and sugar and set it off the dock. The other bags and crates she placed on the dock next to her feet. There wasn't very much and Adrella wondered just how long it would last them. Not very long at all from her reckoning, but she knew Dathan must have worked things out in his mind. He was so very meticulous.

Dathan pulled a Colt revolver from the last crate and stuffed it into the band of his dungarees. Adrella glanced in surprise from the weapon to Dathan. On an isolated island why did he need a gun? Sure there were moccasins and the occasional gator, but they usually stayed more inland near the marshes. Was Dathan expecting some kind of trouble?

She followed him up the beach, carrying the kitten wrapped in the blanket. Since the tide was still out, he chose to follow the beach to the far side of the island instead of going through the woods.

They finally moved out into the open area near the lighthouse. The remnants of their previous camp were still there, the palm frond shelters looking rather worse for wear. They both stopped, each lost in their own memories for a few minutes.

Dathan placed the crate he carried near one of the palm shelters and turned. "I need to prepare the light. If you would like, you can start a fire. There are matches in the crate. Do you remember how?"

Adrella nodded and Dathan headed for the lighthouse. She placed Grace on the sand and watched in amusement as the kitten walked around shaking its paws, obviously not liking the texture of the sand.

"You be good now," she warned.

Adrella gathered some of the dry wood that Dathan had put next to the shelter before they had left the island and loaded it into a pile. It kindled into flame rapidly for which Adrella was grateful. The evening temperatures were dropping quickly.

The light in the tower began to gleam brightly. Before long Dathan joined her, pausing only long enough to tell her, "I need to retrieve the rest of the supplies. I'll be back soon."

He started to move away and Adrella rose to her feet. "I can help."

He glanced from her to the kitten and smiled ruefully. "I think not. It won't take long, but it will still be dark by the time I get finished." He motioned to the crate. "You'll find some sandwiches and fruit in a small wooden box. Help yourself."

Sandwiches? They had to have come from Mrs. Evans, probably when Adrella had gone to change her clothes. The woman's graciousness was the epitome of what she had always thought a minister's wife should be.

Sinking down to the sand, she watched Dathan walk away until he disappeared from sight.

The light from the tower left a reflected glow in the area and brought a calming sense of serenity. It was as though she was back where she was meant to be, like this had always been her life. Her existence before the storm seemed more like an illusion. That life, the life with her Da, she perceived as more akin to a dream than a reality.

Grace was curled up on the quilt asleep. Even the

kitten seemed to sense the peace that had settled down around them.

Adrella dug through the crate to see what it contained. She was surprised at the number of things she discovered. Where on earth had Dathan found all these things?

She pulled an iron tripod from the bottom, one like the soldiers had used during the war and the pioneers had used in their trek across the plains of this country. There was a small kettle to go along with it. She was thrilled with the find. This would have been so useful when they had first been stranded here.

She placed the tripod over the fire and attached the kettle to the hanging handle. Adding water from the canteen, she prepared them some coffee. Although she much preferred tea, she knew Dathan would appreciate the heartier brew.

When she saw him coming up the beach, she poured him a cup. He set a second crate next to the first one and took the cup she handed him. He thanked her with a smile.

"I see you found the coffee. I could smell it coming up the beach."

"Do you want a sandwich?"

He shook his head. "Maybe later. Right now I need to get the rest of the things brought up."

"Are you sure I can't help?"

He shook his head, swallowing the last of his coffee. "No, I can get the rest this next trip."

Adrella glanced at him skeptically. "There doesn't look like much here to last very long."

"There doesn't need to be. I will be going back over in two days."

No wonder the man's muscles looked like something made from granite. Rowing eight miles in a day, and he was going to do it again? She didn't bother to ask why they would need to go back in two days' time. One thing she had learned was that Dathan set his own agenda and, like the hurricane, it was best to bend in the wind if you didn't want to be blown away.

When Dathan left again, Adrella got up and walked down to stand by the shore. The gulf waters lapping against the shore played a soothing cadence of music that filled her with awe. There was water for as far as the eye could see, with unknown beauty and dangers in its depths. She had always loved the gulf, even when it was in a temper.

The flashing rhythm of the light reflected on the surface of the water along with the moon. Stars were beginning to appear in ever-increasing numbers.

She silently watched, feeling closer to God than she had since her Da had died. Scriptures he had made her memorize as a child came back to her now bringing with them the sense of a fate far beyond her control.

Whither shall I go from thy spirit? or whither shall I flee from thy presence? If I ascend up into heaven, thou art there: if I make my bed in hell, behold, thou art there. If I take the wings of the morning and dwell in the uttermost parts of the sea; even there shall thy hand lead me.

"What are you thinking?"

Adrella jumped, giving a slight scream. Her hand covered her chest where her heart thundered against her ribs.

"You scared me half to death!" she admonished.

Dathan gave her an amused smile. "You must have been a hundred miles away."

She turned back to the water, now deep and dark with the absence of sunlight.

"No, not really," she answered softly.

He came closer, placing his hands on her shoulders. Her heart, which had started to slow down to normal, now beat faster.

"Thinking of your father?"

She nodded.

"Me, too," he told her quietly.

They stood for several moments staring out at the water in companionable silence. Dathan finally broke the hush. Squeezing her shoulder, he told her, "Come help me with the tent."

Adrella followed him back to their camp, for the first time hopeful about the future.

Chapter 10

After the tent had been erected, Dathan and Adrella settled down near the fire to eat a late supper.

The sandwiches were of smoked ham and pickles, spread with home-churned butter, a specialty of Mrs. Evans. Adrella licked the residue from her fingers, only now realizing how hungry she had been.

Dathan was reclining on the sand across the fire from her. She handed him an orange and he took it from her, nodding his thanks.

The mosquitoes were finally a diminishing presence due to the changing weather. Adrella hugged her shawl closer against the chill temperature. Dathan noticed and added more wood to the fire, stirring the embers to give it more life.

Grace crawled into Adrella's lap, turned in a circle and settled down. Adrella stroked the kitten's soft fur and smiled at the ensuing purr. She glanced at Dathan and noticed that he seemed relaxed, content, which seemed odd given the circumstances.

She was hesitant to ask, but she knew there were things between them that needed to be brought out into the open. When Dathan had set up the tent, she noticed that he had made two pallets inside.

"Dathan."

She paused, not certain how to put her thoughts into words. His lifted eyebrow encouraged her to continue. Hot color filled her face and she couldn't meet his eyes.

"I'm not certain what you expect of me as a wife," she told him anxiously. Would he understand all the intricacies behind that simple statement? There was so much she was only now beginning to realize that they had never even discussed.

He studied her in silence for several seconds. The fire cast his face in shadows hiding his features from her. Not that she could read them anyway. He was the one with that gift.

Sparks shot up into the air startling her.

Dathan leaned forward and picked up his coffee. "Well, I'm not exactly sure what you expect of me as a husband, either."

Adrella stared at him in surprise. She had been so concerned about herself that she hadn't even given a thought to how he might be feeling at this suddenly arranged marriage. Was he feeling as uncomfortable right now as she was? It was hard to imagine. He was always so self-assured.

Two pallets suggested sleeping apart. Is this what he wanted from their marriage? Did he not want children someday? That was something she longed for with all her heart.

His searching look brought the warmth flooding into

her face again. "You said you trusted me. Then trust me when I say I'm your friend. I would never do anything to harm that friendship."

Whatever was that supposed to mean? He wasn't helping matters any. Such a statement was hardly reassuring. She gave him an unfriendly look.

"Look, Adrella," he said evenly. "I know I rushed you into this marriage. I know I never told you about my past and such but, despite that, I am still, and always will be, your friend. I want what you're willing to give. No more, no less," he said decisively.

She didn't know whether to be relieved by that statement or not.

"Is ours then to be a marriage of convenience?"

She couldn't read the look that passed through his eyes.

"Until we are ready for something more."

What if they were never ready for something more? What if Dathan never grew to love her, what then? She heard him sigh and knew he was reading her thoughts in her face again.

"Adrella, let's just go on as we have been for the past two weeks. We'll let the future take care of itself."

"And your family?" That was her greatest fear.

He frowned. "What about my family?" Seeing her expression, he sat up, his look wandering over her in appraisal. "What exactly are you afraid of?"

"I—I'm not certain what they will expect of your wife."

"Since I doubt we will be seeing them anytime soon, let's cross that bridge when we get to it. I have no intention of returning to New York in the foreseeable future. I am quite content with being a lighthouse keeper."

Adrella looked down, her hair tumbling about her face and hiding the thoughts he could so easily read. "I'm afraid I'll shame you."

He shook his head, smiling. "Never."

He wasn't taking the differences in their status as seriously as she was. After all, he was comfortable with a life of wealth, she was not.

His sigh echoed softly on the night air. "I would expect Mangus Murphy's daughter to have a little more pride in herself."

She jerked her head up, anger sparking in her eyes. "I have plenty of pride in meself!"

"Then act like it, Woman!"

They glared at each other for several seconds. Dathan was the first to crack a smile. They both started laughing and Adrella felt once again the friendship they had shared together before their hasty marriage.

There was so much about Dathan that she didn't know. She wondered just how much he was willing to tell her.

"Why is there such enmity between you and your parents? I would think being an only child, you would have been spoiled."

The look he gave her spoke volumes. "You mean like you?"

Affronted, she sat up straighter and glared at him. "I am not spoiled!"

His eyes danced with laughter. "I was teasing, Adrella."

Recognizing it for the truth, she told him "Sorry." She settled back and apologized with a shrug. In actuality she probably was spoiled. At least a little. All right, maybe more than a little.

Dathan stared into the fire and his face suddenly took on a more serious cast.

"Actually," he told her, "I wasn't always an only child."

Adrella sat forward in surprise, but refrained from comment hoping that he would continue. He did.

"I had a brother and a sister, but my sister died when I

was twelve. She was eight." He paused and Adrella could see he was trying to marshal his thoughts. "Gabriella was a beautiful child, the only girl of my parents and, yes—" he smiled at her "—quite spoiled."

"How did she die?"

"She got influenza. No matter how wealthy you are, disease is no respecter of persons. It's what first made me decide to become a doctor."

He stirred the fire again. Adrella realized that she hadn't even noticed it diminishing, so engrossed had she been in their discussion.

"And your brother? What happened to him? Was he younger than you, too?"

He shook his head. "No, he was actually the eldest. When the war started, he enlisted. My father was furious, but there was no stopping Wyatt. I think he had delusions of grandeur, believing he would be some kind of war hero. More than likely, though, it was just a way to get away from the pressure of our parents. He died at Gettysburg."

It always came back to his parents. The mere mention of them had Adrella's heart thumping irregularly with anxiety.

"In what way did they pressure him?"

He shrugged. "The right clothes, the right wife, the right job. You name it, they meddled in it."

"And you?" she asked softly.

He smiled wryly. "Pretty much the same."

He looked across the fire at her, but his thoughts were turned inward. She could tell it by the way his eyes were glassed over.

"I think my trouble with my parents originated when I became a Christian."

"Your parents aren't Christians?" she asked in surprise.

He shrugged. "Oh, they attend church, if that's what you

mean, but there is no real commitment there. They were appalled when I stopped drinking and began staying home to study more. Dances and soirees no longer appealed to me. I found myself absorbed in medicine, wanting to be a healer like Jesus."

"But surely that's a noble goal," she insisted.

"They had no problem with my becoming a doctor, it was when I decided to follow my brother into battle."

Adrella could well imagine how parents would feel about their child going off to war and possibly never returning.

"That's understandable. They wouldn't want to lose both of their sons after having lost their only daughter."

"I suppose that's true. It's only as I have been here on the island with so much time to think that I realized just how much they loved me. I thought about having children of my own and how I would treat them." Dathan's smile was ironic. "I'm pretty sure I would meddle."

Adrella chuckled. "I'm pretty certain I would as well."

His look became more serious. "And do you want children, Adrella?"

More than anything, she wanted to tell him. Instead she lifted her shoulders in a shrug.

That hadn't really been an answer, but it would have to do for now. He had spoken only of friendship. She wanted so much more than friendship, but she supposed that would have to do for the time being.

She could tell he didn't want to, but he allowed the conversation to drop. He took the kitten from her and helped her to her feet. "Let's get some sleep," he told her. "We have a big day ahead of us."

Adrella had no idea what would constitute a big day when they were the only two people on a tiny island with very few supplies. Shrugging, she preceded Dathan into the tent. He handed her Grace and his eyes met hers briefly.

"Good night, Adrella," he told her softly.

He settled down on his pallet, turning his back to her. She crawled into her own bed, settling Grace next to her, and did likewise.

The next morning when Dathan returned from tending the light, he found Adrella already up and fixing breakfast.

He had started a fire earlier and she was stirring a pot of oatmeal over the flame. She gave him a tentative smile.

"Breakfast will be ready in a few minutes."

He gave a quick nod and climbed into the tent, retrieving the pistol from his bag. He placed it in the band of his pants, covering it with his shirt. No sense in alarming Adrella until it was necessary. They would enjoy a nice breakfast first and maybe finish the conversation Adrella had so quickly terminated last night.

He sat on the ground near the fire. He would be so glad when the supplies arrived. While he was enjoying the time alone with Adrella, he was really getting tired of the lack of amenities. It reminded him a little too much of his time in the army.

Adrella handed him a bowl. "I didn't know if you liked sugar in yours, or not, so I left it plain."

His eyebrows flew to his hairline. "Does anyone eat oatmeal without sugar?"

"Of course." She laughed. "It's the way most Irish do it. A little milk, maybe."

He shook his head, wrinkling his nose. "For future reference—" he cautioned "—I like mine with plenty of brown sugar and lots of butter."

She stared at him in surprise, her fists on her hips. "Butter! Sugar I've heard of, but butter?"

"You eat yours your way, and I'll eat mine my way," he snorted derisively, but there was laughter in his eyes.

She just shook her head and sat down to eat. She had opened a can of milk and had poured a bowl for Grace before she poured her own.

"Adrella," he started and saw her tense at the tone of his voice. Perhaps now was not a good time to continue their conversation from last night, he decided. She was obviously not in a mood for it. He would bide his time, but they would have to continue it sometime. In the meantime he didn't want to rock the boat any further and possibly undo the trust he had garnered in her. He changed his mind about what he was going to say.

"I want you to learn how to care for the light."

Her eyes widened in surprise, her spoon stopped midway to her mouth. "Seriously?"

He nodded, scooping brown sugar into his oatmeal. "I'll take you this morning and show you what to do."

"Why?" she asked uneasily.

He took a deep breath and was unable to meet her look. "I have to return to Apalach tomorrow and I need to be gone overnight. I need you to care for the light while I'm gone."

He glanced back at her and met her appalled look.

"You're leaving me here alone?" she croaked.

"I don't have a choice," he answered, the frustration coming through in his voice. He had tried to reason his way around this action, but had not been able to come up with a solution. He couldn't leave her in Apalach and he couldn't be two places at once. To get things started in regard to supplies, he needed to be on hand.

He sighed heavily. "Adrella, if I thought there was any danger at all, I would never leave you alone here."

Several heartbeats passed before she asked him tonelessly, "If there's no danger, why did you bring a gun?"

He glanced down and saw the gun peeking from his shirt. His eyes shifted to her.

"Honestly, I thought you might feel safer with it."

Her face was ravaged by the fear that he sensed was escalating the more she thought about being alone here. He couldn't blame her, having barely survived a hurricane of enormous magnitude. The dread in her eyes was his undoing. He closed the distance between them, placing his hands on her shoulders reassuringly.

"Never mind. I'll think of something else."

Her face was suddenly void of expression. "It's something you really need to do, isn't it? Something that only you can do."

"Never mind. I'll think of another way."

She shook her head. "No, it's all right. I'll be fine."

His look was skeptical.

"Honestly," she said doggedly.

He rubbed a hand behind his neck trying to ease the tension coiling there. Go, or stay? He couldn't decide which would be better, or which was more necessary.

"Dathan, I'll be fine. You took me by surprise is all."

"I hope I can make it back in time," he told her softly and saw the color drain from her face.

If she had a house to live in, this wouldn't be such a problem. But living in a tent? He could foresee all kinds of problems. Did she see them as well?

She glanced around at their small camp. Her shoulders set resolutely.

"I can do it. At least the hurricane season is nearly past, so I won't have that to worry with. Show me how to care for the light. The sooner you go, the sooner you'll be back."

Dathan lifted his eyes heavenward, closing them and

gritting his teeth. He just knew this wasn't a good idea, but what choice did he have? Without the money, he couldn't begin the house; without the house he couldn't begin to build their new life.

He had made a promise, and he intended to keep it. For the time being he would have to leave Adrella's protection up to God, who he was certain was infinitely more capable than he was.

Carrying Grace, Adrella reluctantly followed Dathan into the light tower. She lifted prayers heavenward as she slowly climbed the iron stairs to the top. She shivered slightly and not from the cold. This place held a lot of bad memories, but conversely, it held some good ones as well. Though, truth be told, the bad far outweighed the good.

Dathan showed her where all the supplies were kept and taught her how to light the wick inside the lens. He carefully explained the procedures and she listened just as carefully, memorizing all the little details. She wouldn't let him down. If he could live on this island alone for two years, she could certainly last a few days.

And nights, her mind prompted and she quickly hushed it into silence. If a person once let insidious thoughts enter his mind, they could quickly incapacitate him. She refused to allow that to happen. Too often she had refused to act because of some fear on her part. It showed a decided lack of faith in God and He had shown Himself to be her protector already. He wouldn't let her down.

"Remember," he instructed, "always wear the apron when anywhere near the lens. And under no circumstances use a buff skin that has been wet as it will scratch the lens."

She glanced at all the supplies needed to maintain just the lens and looked at him fearfully. There was a lot to remember.

He took her by the shoulders, bending until he could look into her face.

"You'll be fine. All the instructions are written in this book." He reached over and lifted the book from the shelf where it rested. "I have faith in you."

That was all well and good, but did she have faith in herself? She straightened her shoulders, hiding her misgivings with a smile. There had been many lightkeepers that were women. Even at the St. Marks Light north of here Mrs. Dudley had been a keeper for several years. If Mrs. Dudley could do it, then she certainly could.

Looking relieved, Dathan returned her smile.

"I've already checked all the clock mechanisms and machinery, so don't worry about anything except the daily duties of lighting the light and polishing the lens."

He released her and started to descend the stairs. She followed him down. At least she would have something to do while he was gone.

"Now," he said as they exited the tower. "It's time to teach you how to use the gun."

Chapter 11

After extinguishing the light, Adrella hung the lantern curtains and began to put the apparatus in order for re-lighting. She carefully covered the illuminating apparatus before starting to clean the Fresnel lens.

She picked up the feather brush to remove any dust, and wondered for the hundredth time how much longer Dathan would be. He had said overnight, and it had been five.

What if something had happened to him? How would anyone even know that she was here?

She used the soft linen cloth on the lens to give it a slight polish before she reached for the buff skin.

Her overactive imagination had been working over-time while here on the island alone, especially at night. The loneliness would be enough to drive someone mad, at least someone like her. It hadn't taken her very long to realize that it took someone special to be a lightkeeper.

How had Dathan endured the solitude? At times when

he had come to the store she thought she had sensed his loneliness, but he never mentioned it to her or her father. As for herself, it wouldn't take much to make her dive into the gulf and try to reach the mainland. She would definitely be one of those who went insane. She had done a lot of chatting to Grace in the past few days, thankful that she at least had the kitten for company.

She couldn't allow the kitten with her when tending the light so she always placed her in one of the empty crates. Grace, having learned to accept the situation, would curl into a ball on the quilt Adrella had brought with her, and sleep. In truth, the kitten slept a lot, more than likely due to poor health from the lack of sustenance it had received. Already Grace's little body was beginning to fill out some from the extra canned milk Adrella had been giving her.

After she finished cleaning the light, Adrella exited the lighthouse as quickly as possible. It still bothered her to be in such a confined space, although focusing on the job of tending the light helped to take her mind off it.

Adrella wandered down to the beach, lifting a hand to shield her eyes from the bright sunlight so that she could see across the water to the mainland. Nothing moved on the water, not even the ever-frolicking dolphins.

Dark clouds were building in the east, a presage of an approaching storm. She shivered, and not only from the morning chill. Being alone on this island in good weather was one thing, facing a storm was quite another.

Tugging her shawl closer, she hurried back to the campsite to prepare in case the bad weather made its way to land. For now, it was a long way off and Adrella prayed fervently that it would stay that way.

They were the motliest looking crew of men he had ever seen. Dathan looked over the assemblage of men that had responded to the telegrams from Mr. Carson and Mr. Panganopolis. Some were here about the job at the lighthouse, some in answer to the summons about working in the mill.

Mr. Carson had already vetted some of the men and Dathan had them follow him to a small room at the back of the mill that Mr. Panganopolis used as his own office. The final say of who would go or stay would be left up to Dathan. Although he trusted Mr. Carson, he would trust his own intuition better, his instincts about people having never failed him yet.

He seated himself behind a small desk and motioned the first man forward, a giant man with curling red hair. He had to be well over six feet, his large girth adding to the impression of a mountain of a man. He was twisting his hat in his hands nervously as he approached.

"What can I do for you, Mr.…?"

"Doyle. Sean Doyle. I'm here about the lighthouse job."

Dathan reached out a hand and Sean took it, the surprise evident on his face at the gentlemanly action afforded to him.

"Have you had experience in such work, Mr. Doyle?"

"Not really. In Ireland we build our homes of rock and thatch, but I don't think working with planks would be much different."

Dathan summed him up in a glance, impressed with his honesty. The man's brown eyes were clear of guile. Dathan had a good feeling about him and he was certain Adrella would approve. Sean's Irish brogue was much thicker than Adrella's, but since she had lived in the States for most of her life it was no wonder.

Dathan wrote a note on a piece of paper and handed it to Sean. "Give this to Mr. Carson. He will tell you what to do next."

Sean's eyes gleamed with appreciation. "Thank ya, sir. You'll no be regrettin' it."

Dismissing him with a smile, Dathan motioned the next man forward. If he could be called a man. The young man who stepped up had probably barely started to shave.

"Name?"

"Henry Pierson, sir."

What was Carson thinking sending him such a young man? He studied Henry for a moment, impressed with his quiet reserve. Brown curly hair flowed about his head in wild abandon. Blue eyes quietly studied him back.

Dathan reached a hand forward and Henry took it, his handshake firm. One could tell a lot about a man just by his handshake. Dathan was impressed once again.

"What brings you here, Mr. Pierson?"

The boy looked down at his feet. "If you please, sir. I'm my mother's only means of support, and I have three sisters to boot."

Intrigued, Dathan asked him, "Where are you from, Henry?"

"New York, sir."

Could the boy not find work in New York? Dathan had no idea what in the boy's past had sent him so far from home when he had a family to care for, but he understood Mr. Carson's choice a little better now. Despite his gruff exterior, Carson was a godly man with a heart of gold. Carson was giving the boy a chance and Dathan decided he could do no less. He quickly wrote a note and handed it to Henry.

"Find Mr. Carson."

The boy's head snapped up, his face flushed with relief. "Thank you, sir."

One after another the men came forward. Carson had

done a fine job choosing these men. There wasn't a man among them that Dathan thought to decline.

In the end he had seven men ready to go with him to Cape St. George. With so much help, it shouldn't take long to get the keeper's cottage built. He was suddenly antsy with anticipation. He had been gone from the island for five days now instead of the one he had hoped to be gone. He wanted to get back quickly, but he still had things to see to before they could depart. The delay was frustrating him. He would never forgive himself if something happened to Adrella because of all these delays.

Placing Grace inside the tent, Adrella quickly moved the remaining supplies up to the light tower. If it did rain, it was going to cool the temperature dramatically, especially at night. It would be better to store some dry wood in the tower for protection against the elements so that she would be able to have a fire.

She was perspiring heavily by the time she was finished. Wiping a hand across her brow, she noted that the clouds had steadily moved closer. It looked like she was going to get wet after all.

She moved into the tent with Grace as the first spattering of raindrops hit. The sound grew louder as the rain increased in tempo. The wind shook the tent, but not violently as she had anticipated. She relaxed slightly. It was only a small autumn storm.

Lifting Grace from the crate, she hugged the kitten close. The ensuing purr helped to settle Adrella's nerves.

"Well," she told the kitten, "it looks like we're stuck here for a while."

The drumming of the rain added to her sleepless nights began to make her drowsy. She curled down into her sleeping pallet, Grace tucked against her chest. Before long, her eyes drifted closed and she slept. Sometime later the increasing cold awakened Adrella. The rain had slackened but was still pelting the tent in a steady beat. Shivering, she added Dathan's quilt to her own and huddled down once again.

How many hours had passed? There was no way to tell when dusk was falling because it was already twilight with the darkness of the passing storm and she had no timepiece to give her the hour.

She decided to light the light early. Placing Grace back in her crate, Adrella pulled Dathan's Macintosh from the one crate she had left packed. The coat engulfed her, making it hard to move. Still, it was better than getting soaked and possibly taking a chill.

After entering the tower, she removed the rubber coat and laid it on an oil barrel at the base of the stairs.

Climbing the stairs once again, she couldn't help but think of Dathan doing the same thing twice a day, day after day. The monotony, the boredom, the loneliness, how did he manage to do it for two years? And he didn't even have a kitten to keep him company.

She lit the lantern and leaned against the outside glass of the lantern room trying to see out across the water. The rain against the glass distorted the view. She could see nothing. Sighing, she retraced her steps and returned to the tent.

Leaving the wet coat by the entry, she once again settled down on her pallet. Since Grace was curled up asleep, Adrella left her alone. Shivering, she pulled the quilts over her and fought the tears that threatened.

How much longer, Dathan? She wondered.

The rain continued, once again lulling Adrella to sleep.

* * *

Dathan found Mr. Carson and Mr. Panganopolis at the dock loading the planking onto a small scow that would be used to take all the supplies he had ordered to the island at one time.

Mr. Panganopolis tucked his thumbs into his overall straps. "This'll get you started. I'll have another load to send in about three days."

Dathan nodded. "Good." He had arranged for the funds to be sent down from New York to the bank. Now he needed to see about finding the other supplies he had special ordered. They were supposed to have been delivered to Mr. Yankton's warehouse as soon as possible. They were being shipped over from Mobile so it shouldn't take long but, then again, the whole coast along the gulf had been hit pretty hard by the hurricane. Even with money the appropriations had been difficult.

Mr. Carson handed him a package wrapped in brown paper and twine. Dathan lifted an eyebrow in query.

"It's a flag. I noticed that the other one was missing."

Relieved, Dathan took the package from him. There were specific instructions for lighthouse keepers about keeping the colors. It had bothered him more than a little bit that he hadn't been able to fulfill those obligations.

"When will we be ready to leave?" Mr. Carson asked. He intended to go to the island with them for one last inspection before he headed back north.

"It's too late to do so today," Dathan told him, noticing the descending sun. "We'll leave first thing in the morning."

"I'll be ready."

Shaking hands, Dathan then left to check on the supplies coming into Yankton's warehouse.

He found Mr. Yankton checking a list against the barrels and crates stacked around him. Mr. Yankton looked up and smiled.

"Looks like everything's here, Mr. Adams."

He handed the bill of lading to Dathan and Dathan ran his own inventory. He relaxed when he realized that it was, indeed, complete, even down to the potbellied stove he had requisitioned.

"Good job, Mr. Yankton. Could you send everything down to the dock to be loaded onto the scow? I want to leave as early as possible in the morning."

"Will do. Sorry it took so long."

So was Dathan, but he knew it couldn't be helped. He only hoped Adrella understood and that she was doing okay. Any number of things could go wrong and it had caused him many sleepless nights. The rain last night had him worried.

He moved down to the dock, waiting rather impatiently as the sun dropped lower behind the horizon. He held his breath without realizing it, his heart beating an erratic rhythm.

Each night he had come to this very spot and looked toward the island eight miles away. Each night he waited patiently for the light to shine, the only sign he had that everything was all right with Adrella. Each night he prayed harder than he had ever prayed in his life.

Moments later the light from the lighthouse beamed out across the water. Blowing out a breath in relief, Dathan smiled.

"That's my girl."

He headed back to Mr. Panganopolis's mill where he had made camp for the past several days.

The next morning, Dathan tried to will the boats to go faster. The scow was being towed by two rowboats. One boat held the crew for the lighthouse, the other contained hired men who would then return the emptied scow back to Apalach for another load of planks. Both were rowing steadily toward the island, but not fast enough to check Dathan's impatience.

Adrella was not at the top of the lighthouse. Had she seen them? Was she even now making her way to the dock that serviced the island?

When they finally were close enough, he could see Adrella standing at the small pier waiting for them. His heart jumped, then steadied into a rapid beat.

The closer they came, the harder he studied her. Was she all right? He could see no signs that anything had happened to her physically. Relieved, his shoulders relaxed.

He noticed the men staring at her in various degrees of astonishment.

"My wife," he told them, his voice holding a warning.

They glanced at him in surprise. No wonder, for he had neglected to mention Adrella to them. At the time he had been so focused on other things it hadn't occurred to him.

He glanced back at Adrella and realized just how much he had missed her. He wasn't quite certain what kind of greeting he was going to get. He had promised her one night alone and instead it had been five. She would be within her rights if she lambasted him up one side and down the other. He couldn't help but grin at the thought.

When they were close enough, he jumped from the boat and slogged his way to shore leaving the men to dock the boat. He walked slowly toward Adrella, doubtful of his welcome.

She hesitated but a moment and then ran and threw herself into his arms. Taken by surprise, all he could do was hold her, and it suddenly occurred to him that this was the very thing he most wanted to do.

He tilted her chin up until he could see those glorious green eyes, those eyes that had haunted his sleep for the past several nights. He frowned at the tears that were turning them into a liquid sea.

"Are you all right?" he asked huskily.

"I am now." She smiled, rubbing the tears from her eyes. "What took you so long?"

No recriminations, just an acceptance of his delay and, in her eyes, a delight to see him. He wanted nothing more right now than to stand here holding her and absorb that fact. A cough from behind reminded him of the others' presence.

He placed an arm around her waist and moved her toward the pier. "The hurricane affected many parts of the South. Transportation was sporadic. It took time to get all the supplies together."

They joined Mr. Carson at the pier. He smiled at Adrella.

"Hello again, Mrs. Adams."

Adrella returned his smile. "And to you, Mr. Carson."

"Your husband here was most anxious to get back to you," he said, and Adrella turned Dathan's way, her look one of surprise.

Dathan didn't bother to comment. "Did everything go okay? Did you have a problem with the rain?"

The look that flashed through her eyes was quickly veiled, leaving him to wonder.

"No. No problems."

"I noticed you lit the light early yesterday."

She shrugged, glancing from Dathan to the inspector. "I didn't have a timepiece and it was already getting dark. Was that okay?" she asked lamely.

Dathan frowned. He should have left her his pocket watch.

"Very okay," Mr. Carson answered her. "You did a fine job, Mrs. Adams. But then I wouldn't have expected otherwise. Anyone who can survive a hurricane the way you did obviously has plenty of grit."

Dathan saw that Adrella was pleased with the compliment. He latched on to her hand and pulled her toward the waiting men.

"Let me introduce you to the men who will be helping me build our new home."

Adrella hung back, glancing down at her disheveled appearance. The dress that he had bought her so recently now looked worn and bedraggled. He had to agree that she looked less than presentable, yet he didn't care. He was just glad to see her.

"Come on."

She allowed him to lead her forward and introduce her to the men.

Dathan watched carefully to see if any of them showed anything other than the proper respect, but they each reacted with various shades of shyness when presented to her. He allowed himself to relax.

The men from the other boat had already begun unloading the supplies. Dathan joined them.

"We need to put together the cart I brought with the supplies. We'll use that to move the supplies up to the light. We'll have to go by way of the beach, we'll never make it through the woods."

Adrella joined him and he smiled. "But first things first."

Dathan took a crowbar and began prying open one of the smaller crates. Curious, Adrella came over, impatient to see what was inside. He pulled off the top slats of wood and set them aside. Reaching inside, he lifted out a black cloak complete with hood and lined with fur.

Shaking it out, he stepped over to Adrella and placed it around her shoulders.

"For you. The shawl is hardly warm enough with the temperatures dropping."

A smile of delight crept over her face. "It's beautiful, Dathan! I've never seen anything so beautiful." She rubbed her hands down the soft wool. "And so warm."

He gathered the ribbon ties at the neck and knotted them into a bow. Holding the collar, he lifted her chin with his thumbs until he could see her eyes.

"I'm glad you like it," he told her huskily.

He caught his breath at the look she returned. "I love it. Thank you," she assured him softly. His eyes fastened on her lips and, at her slight catch of breath, his pulse jumped sending blood through his veins like liquid fire.

"Cap'n, where you want we should put these?"

Startled, Dathan dropped his hands and stepped back. His dazed look turned to the man who had spoken.

"What?"

The other man glanced from him to Adrella and Dathan wanted to knock the smirk from his face. Dathan was glad the man was with the other crew or else he would have fired him on the spot.

"These barrels of flour. Where do you want them?"

Dathan gave the man a glare that had the effect of cowing him into silence.

"Just put everything on the beach and my men and I will handle it from there."

"Aye, sir." Recognizing the ire he had engendered, he glanced apologetically at Dathan before moving away.

Dathan shook himself from his angry mood and turned back to Adrella. She was studying him in bewilderment. Somehow he thought Mangus must have neglected her education when it came to men. He was going to have to rectify that as soon as possible.

He held out his hand and she placed hers in it and he tugged her over to the supplies.

"There's more in the container. That entire crate is for you."

Her look of astonishment brought a smile to his face. She pulled out a yellow taffeta dress with a blue lace overskirt. She shook it out and held it against her and he thought how magnificent she would look strolling in his parents' garden in New York.

She carefully folded the garment and placed the dress back inside the crate, her face devoid of emotion.

"I'll wait until we have a house before wearing these things."

Her voice lacked animation and for the first time he couldn't read what was in her face. He was surprised at the wave of disappointment he felt, even though it made perfect sense that she would want to wait to wear the garments. He wondered at her lack of enthusiasm. Did she not like the clothes?

"That's a good idea," he agreed carefully. He motioned to the men unloading the cargo.

"We'll have a hungry horde to feed. Think you can do it?"

She watched the supplies being unloaded, enough to feed a small army. She smiled slightly.

"We'll soon find out."

Chapter 12

Adrella watched men scampering up the scaffolding that lined the side of her soon-to-be new home. Since most of the coast had suffered severe damage from the hurricane, the Lighthouse Board had commissioned men from other communities to help repair the damage done to the lighthouses along the gulf. Dathan had used his money to make certain that theirs was one of the first.

Her attention was caught by her husband's form as he hoisted lumber to the men working on the roof. She studied his sun-bronzed figure, perspiration drenching his white cotton shirt, and sighed.

They had been married for two weeks now, yet she still didn't feel like a wife. Dathan was courteous and respectful, all the things she had come to expect of him over the years, yet he held himself aloof. Distant.

He had declined to leave her behind when he returned to the island. Hearing some of the comments, and finally noticing some of the looks they were being given, she thought she understood. She wanted to protest that they had done nothing wrong, but she knew that would do little good. Once people had made up their minds about such things, there was usually no changing them.

She sat down next to the light tower, leaning her back against its smooth surface. The cold from the building crept through her clothing, adding to the already chill temperatures. November had proceeded with a devastating cold spell that left people shaking their heads over the strange weather. She pulled her cape close around her shoulders thankful for its warmth.

The garment was beautiful as well as useful, but far fancier than anything she would have ever considered for herself. As were the other dresses in the crate he had brought for her. She felt like Dathan was trying to change her into something she was not and never could be.

For a long time she watched the men as they went about their business. A nippy breeze lifted her heavy hair from her shoulders and she leaned her head back enjoying the feel of the cooling temperatures against her neck.

Although they had a tent for their use until the house was built, she had no desire to stay within its hot confines during the beautiful days. Several other tents that had been set up by the workers were scattered around the beach. They would remain there until the house was finished. Adrella could hardly wait for that day to come, not because she didn't enjoy the company, but because she would finally have her own home.

She wanted so much to have time with Dathan, his attention not divided among the myriad jobs to be overseen. It became a fixed idea in her head that when they had time alone she could make him fall in love with her. She knew he was attracted to her physically, but that wasn't enough.

She wanted them to be one in mind as well as body. To share souls.

Shaking herself from her melancholy mood, she tried to think of something she might do to occupy her time. She was feeling decidedly unproductive these days. There was really nothing that she could do to help, and she was growing irritable over her boredom.

Getting to her feet, she strolled down to the water, ambling along the shoreline. As she meandered by the water's edge, she added shells to her fast-growing collection, fascinated by their colors and shapes. She kept a careful watch to make certain that she didn't come into contact with any more jellyfish that might have washed up on the shore.

When she finally noticed the waning of the afternoon sun, she retraced her steps and returned to their camp. It was time to prepare the evening meal. That, at least, was one thing she could do well.

After she had served all the workers, she took her own plate and retired to a spot near the fire in front of her and Dathan's tent. He joined her there moments later.

His eyes rested on her briefly before he focused his attention on his plate. He lifted a spoon of the stew, motioning in her direction.

"The men really appreciate your cooking for them. Otherwise they would probably make do with hardtack and a little meat."

Adrella lifted her chin slightly. "It's the least I can do. There's not much else to occupy my time."

He lifted his gaze, frowning. "Give us time, Drell. We'll have you a home before long."

She sighed, scraping her stew with a biscuit. "I'm sorry, Dathan. I'm not complaining, really." She lifted her eyes to meet his. "I just feel so useless."

She saw his lips tilt into a one sided smile. "Haven't you ever heard that a woman's job is just to look beautiful?"

Blowing out through her lips, Adrella rose to her feet. "Then I'm for certain useless."

Dathan rose to his feet also, his eyes narrowed to slits. "Why do you do that?"

"Do what?"

"Talk about yourself that way," he reprimanded, taking her plate from her hand and adding it to his own.

She shrugged. "I don't know. It's true."

Setting the plates on a tree stump, Dathan stepped toward her, taking her by the shoulders. "I don't know what you're comparing yourself to, but you have a beauty all your own," he said gruffly. He began to massage her shoulders with his thumbs, his gaze capturing hers. "Your eyes are so green, they put the Emerald Isle to shame." His hands slid up to frame her face. "Your skin is so white, it reminds me of new fresh cream, rich and delicious." His voice grew huskier by the minute, and Adrella swallowed hard. "Your dark red hair shimmers in the firelight with golden highlights, almost as though it had a life of its own," he told her softly, one finger twisting around a curling lock. The pupils of his eyes were dilated until the only thing she could see was her own reflection. She thought he was going to kiss her; in fact she *hoped* that he would, but he released her suddenly. "If that's not beauty, then I don't know what is."

Picking up the plates, he turned and left her staring after him, her mouth hanging open and her heart thundering in her chest.

Adrella turned for the hundredth time on her mat, pulling her quilt up to her chin. Sleep was elusive tonight.

She could hear Dathan's soft breathing across from her,

telling her that he was deeply asleep. Sighing, she tried to be still. How could the man calmly shatter her world, and then go to sleep as though nothing momentous had occurred?

Punching her pillow, she glared into the darkness. Perhaps his words had meant nothing to *him,* but to her they had meant everything. The timbre of his voice had sent her blood racing through her veins, her hopes soaring.

She tossed and turned until she could see faint sunlight filtering through the cracks in the tent, and still she had resolved nothing in her own mind.

She could hear Dathan stirring on his mat and knew that the day would soon begin. Getting to her feet, she went outside to prepare breakfast. Taking the time to wash her face first, she noticed how cold the water was in the bucket. If they didn't hurry with the house, they would be spending their nights in some rather cold temperatures.

Dathan joined her a few moments later, watching as she stirred the batter for flapjacks. He glanced to the rising wood structure that would one day be their home.

"A few more days should do it."

Adrella nodded, adding batter to the grease in the sizzling cast iron skillet. The wood burning stove seemed rather incongruous among all the tents and small fires, but Adrella was grateful for it nevertheless. Dathan had managed to scrounge up any number of supplies to keep them until the house was built. His resourcefulness was a constant amazement to her.

The men began wandering into their camp, a ragged bunch of hooligans. Adrella smiled to herself at the thought. They might look like a bunch of ruffians, but they had hearts of pure gold. Each man treated her as though she were some precious gem, and over the past few weeks she had become very fond of them.

One man, Smiley, sauntered up to Adrella now, his shaggy dark hair ruffled from sleep standing in spikes about his head. He grinned at Adrella. "Howdy, ma'am. Sure smells good."

Adrella handed him a plate, returning his smile. "Thanks, Smiley. Help yourself to the molasses."

After everyone had been served, Dathan excused himself to return to his duties at the light. After he finished that, he would join the men in working on the house. It was no surprise to Adrella that he practically fell into bed each night.

She took her dishes down to the water and rinsed them out. Having done that, she would have most of the day to spend by herself again. Wrinkling her nose, she wished that something would happen to change her monotony.

Only hours later she would regret that thought when one of the men almost severed his arm at the elbow.

His screams brought Adrella running. She forced her way through the crowd of men standing around and found Dathan kneeling beside the young man named Henry. The sight that met her eyes brought the bile rising to her throat.

"What happened?" she asked, her voice barely above a whisper. Dathan took one look at her white face and told her to sit down.

"He was working the saw. His arm slipped," he told her, his voice clipped as he tied a tourniquet above Henry's elbow. "I need to sew it back together."

"Can you do that?"

Adrella didn't see how anyone could save the mangled piece of flesh that hung by a mere thread.

"I've got to try." Adrella recognized the steel that threaded through his words. There really was no option. The nearest doctor was in Apalach, and after the hurricane's destruction, he was no better equipped than they.

"I need boiling water and clean cloths. Help me get him into his tent. And bring me a light."

The staccato orders sent everyone scampering to do his bidding.

"Adrella," he turned to her. "In the lighthouse is my case of instruments. Get them. And for the love of heaven, hurry."

She ran to do as told, praying all the way. Henry was such a good boy and his mother's only source of income. She would be devastated if something couldn't be done for him.

"Please, God. Let him live!"

When she returned to the tent, Dathan had already set up to do surgery. Adrella could see the dread in his face and swallowed hard.

"I want you out of here," he told her roughly.

She fixed him with a glare. "I can help," she argued.

"I have all the help I need. You'll only be in the way. Please leave."

He focused his look on Sean. "I don't have any chloroform."

Sean's face went from shock to tight-lipped acceptance as he scrutinized young Henry writhing in agony.

Adrella recognized that messages were passing between the men's eyes and she had no problem interpreting them. Henry would be awake through the surgery. Her stomach began to churn even faster.

"Adrella, I'll need Keith. Find him and send him here, and then leave." There was no gainsaying the command in his voice.

She understood then. Keith was second only to Sean in size and strength. They would be needed to hold Henry down.

Henry began to moan quietly. "Please don't cut off my arm. Please!"

"Hurry, Adrella."

Adrella didn't have far to look. All the men were gathered outside the tent awaiting word.

"Keith, Dathan needs you."

Startled, Keith hesitated but a second before quickly passing Adrella and vanishing inside the tent.

Adrella peered inside, intent on helping in some way. She saw Sean raise a beefy fist and slam it into Henry's jaw. Henry's body went slack. The bile she had been struggling with refused to be denied any longer. Ducking outside the tent, Adrella quickly hurried away and wretched, her stomach heaving.

She sank to her knees, the horror of this day bringing tears to her eyes. "Dear God," she prayed. "Please let Dathan save Henry, if not his arm, then at least his life. Please! I'm begging you, in Jesus's name."

She stayed there for some time petitioning the Lord on the young man's behalf. And then she added prayers for Dathan, realizing how this must be resurrecting the memories he had tried so hard to obliterate from his mind.

She finally joined the other men outside the tent to await any news. They threw her sympathetic looks, and she was fairly certain that more than one of them wished they could have joined her in losing their supper.

They knew the moment that Henry awoke from Sean's imposed sedation, his screams filling the air.

Hours later Henry lay unconscious with his arm bandaged and in a sling. Dathan had been thankful when the boy had finally passed out and he had been able to finish the tedious job of putting his arm back together without his screams filling the tent.

Sean and Keith dropped to the ground, the sweat running in rivulets down their faces despite the cold temperatures. Keith was visibly shaking.

"Thank the good Lord that's over," Sean breathed, glancing at Dathan. "Do you think he'll live?"

Worry lines etched across Dathan's brow. "Time will tell. We need to get him to the mainland, to the nearest city with a hospital."

Smiley peered inside the tent having overheard their conversation. "We'll take him, Cap'n."

Nodding, Dathan helped the men prepare Henry for travel. He only hoped the boy would stay unconscious. It was a long eight miles to the mainland.

"Use the skiff, it will be faster," he told them.

It was a solemn group of men that set off through the woods.

When the rest of the crew gathered for supper that night, Adrella missed Smiley's cheerful face. The old man was always joking and laughing. There was an ominous quiet about the remaining men.

Sean glanced across at Dathan, his face full of respect.

"I've never seen anythin' like what you did today. You pieced poor Henry's arm back together like it was a bit of quilt."

Adrella heard the mumbles of assent from those present and had to agree. She had never seen anything quite like it herself. Her gaze fixed on her husband. He had an incredible gift from God. He should be using it to help others, not hiding away on this remote island.

He glanced her way, and as though he could read her thoughts, his lips thinned with displeasure and he turned away.

"It may not work," Dathan rebutted.

Sean shrugged, holding his hands out to the fire. "Maybe not, but it's not for want of tryin'."

Later, when they crawled into their beds that night, Adrella sat up and addressed her husband.

"Dathan, you have such a gift. Why aren't you using that gift to help others?"

He turned his back to her, burrowing under his own quilt. "I already told you."

Undaunted, she moved closer so that he could better hear her without her having to raise her voice.

"I know. You gave up on people, not on God." She had a hard time trying to keep the censure from her voice. "But Dathan, don't you remember what Jesus said? To seek and save the lost?"

Dathan didn't answer her, but through the dim light afforded by the fire outside she could see him stiffen.

"Dathan," she countered softly. "When you give up on people, you *are* giving up on God. We are *all* God's children. Where would you be now if Jesus had felt the same about us. About you."

He slowly turned to face her, and through the darkness she could see that he was listening intently.

"Do you remember the parable that Jesus told about the men with the talents?" she asked.

His lips pressed tightly together. "I remember."

"Although the talents spoken of there refer to money, the principle is still the same," she told him. "God has given you an incredible gift, and you are burying it in the sand."

Dathan sat up, pushing one hand back through his hair. His eyes glittered at her through the darkness. "That's enough, Adrella."

She wanted to argue with him more, but she could see that her words had struck their mark. Now she needed to let him think about what she had said. Still, she offered one more bit of wisdom.

"When the hurricane hit and my da…my da died…my faith was shaken. It was shaken again when I knew I had lost everything. I began to doubt God. But do you know what? He sent me *you*. He sent you to take care of me when I thought I had no one, and then I realized that He hadn't really given up on me at all." She reached across the space between them and touched the gold band on Dathan's hand. Her father's ring fit his finger perfectly. "Me da knew you were a good man, Dathan. He wouldn't have trusted me to just anyone."

Dathan stared at her through the darkness and knew that in a sense she was right. Without conceit, he knew that few people could have done what he did today. It was a humbling thought, though, to know that his skill came not from anything of his own, but rather from God Himself. In the end, regardless of what he might know or what he could do, God's will would prevail.

Adrella pulled back, settling down under her quilt. She turned her back to him and left him alone with his chaotic thoughts.

He felt responsible. Henry was just a boy. He shouldn't have entrusted him with such a dangerous job. The boy was his mother's only means of support. He had no idea if his surgery would keep the boy from losing that arm. There were too many variables.

Doing surgery in a tent. The memories came back to haunt him once again. How many people had he watched die because of the same primitive conditions?

Yet, at the same time, how many people had he helped to save? Why was it that a loss seemed more profound than a win?

He should have gone with the boy. Things had happened so fast, he hadn't considered it at the time. There was no way that he would leave Adrella here on the island alone with four men, and the skiff wouldn't have held them all. Still, he should have gone.

He could hear Adrella's soft breathing telling him that she was fast asleep. Her faith in him made him want to live up to her expectations. He wished he could say that he had as much faith in himself.

What was he to do? Her words had brought him up short. To give up on mankind was to give up on God. He had never seen it that way before. All this time he had thought himself so spiritual. By walking away from his fellow man he had, in truth, walked away from God. He had denied the gift that God had given him, that gift that was made to help those created in His image.

It was no good trying to hide from God. He could run and he could try to hide, but it was useless. He could hide from himself maybe, but that was about the extent of it.

It was time to quit running.

Chapter 13

Dathan watched the sun rise in glorious shades of pink, orange and yellow. The beauty didn't fool him, though, for the colors were precursors of a storm to come. He only hoped it would avoid his little island.

He pulled back the flap on his tent and ducked his head inside. Adrella slept peacefully, curled into a small ball, one hand resting beneath her cheek the other on the cat. Heavy red lashes fanned out across her creamy pale cheeks, her breathing soft and even.

The picture she made drew him inside, and he hunkered down next to her sleeping form. The innocent image caused such a wave of tenderness to swamp him that he could hardly breathe.

He had tried to fight it but there was no denying the feelings that coursed through him. He was in love with his little wife. The question was, what exactly did she feel about him? He could tell that she was attracted to him, but was that just a small feeling of gratitude for what he had done for her?

The day before yesterday he had almost kissed her again. That's when he knew. His whole world had suddenly turned upside down. The feelings had crept up on him so slowly that he had been unaware they were even there. The look she had given him had made him wish they were alone on the island, or anywhere for that matter. He sighed. Maybe it was a good thing they weren't.

"Adrella," he called softly.

She stretched like a sleek cat, her eyes blinking drowsily up at him. Her rosy lips curled up into a smile.

"Good morning."

"Good morning, yourself." He grinned. "I hate to bother you, but the men are waiting for their breakfast."

Eyes going wide, Adrella sat up quickly. "Oh my. I overslept!"

"Don't feel badly about it," Dathan told her. "I think everyone had trouble sleeping last night. They are very fond of young Henry."

Adrella knew that was certainly true. Being the youngest, the other men treated him much like a younger brother, or in the cases of some, more like a son.

She allowed Dathan to help her to her feet. His eyes slowly went over the nightdress he had brought her, bringing color rushing to her face despite the fact that it was made of yards and yards of material and hid every inch of her body.

"I'll be outside," he said dryly.

Making a hasty toilette, she hurried to feed the men.

His frown told her that Dathan noted she had changed into one of the new dresses, one less fancy and made for day wear. He said nothing, just looked at her quizzically.

She knew that he had been disappointed in her reaction to the new clothes, but she couldn't help it. She would have much preferred dresses more appropriate to her position here on the island. She was uncomfortable in the fine clothes, clothes she felt she could never live up to.

While she was frying the flapjacks, Sean came over to talk to Dathan. Doffing his cap respectfully, he nervously cleared his throat. Dathan instantly gave him his attention.

"Cap'n, I'd like to speak with you a moment."

The men called him captain after finding out that he had that rank in the war.

Dathan nodded, and he continued. "Well, it's like this. The men and me, we figured since young Henry won't be able to work for a while, and since he was the only means of support for his mama, well, we figure we'd like to help out."

Sean finished this rush of words by coloring hotly. Ducking his head slightly, he twisted his hat in his hands.

Dathan laid a hand on his shoulder, squeezing reassuringly. These men made such a show of being tough, but anyone who knew them knew that they had very large hearts, especially concerning one of their own.

"What do you want to do?" Dathan asked.

Looking relieved, Sean pulled a large roll of bills and coins from his pocket. "The men and me, we took up this collection. We wondered if you could get it to Henry whilst we finish your house here."

She could see Dathan swallow the lump in his throat. Adrella hastily brushed the tears from her own face.

"Mrs. Adams and I will see to it right away," he told Sean huskily.

Grinning from ear to ear, the big man shook Dathan's hand.

"Thanks, Cap'n."

Adrella watched him hurry away to tell the others. Dathan cocked a brow at Adrella. "Is that all right with you, Mrs. Adams?"

She smiled her answer. Nodding slightly, Dathan picked his cap off a rock, dusting it against his trousers.

"Then I'll see about getting the light in order so we can leave as soon as possible. We need to be back before evening."

It took most of the day for them to reach Henry's location since he had been ferried inland to a hospital untouched by the hurricane. The little hospital was packed wall-to-wall with people from the surrounding communities devastated by the storm. Henry's mother was sitting at his side holding his good hand. Henry was still unconscious, more than likely due to the drugs he would have been given for the pain.

Dathan placed a hand on his brow and Adrella searched Dathan's face for a clue to Henry's condition. Dathan stepped back, nodding his head in satisfaction.

"No fever so far. That's good."

Adrella noticed the quizzical look Mrs. Pierson was giving them. She stepped to her side.

"Mrs. Pierson, my name is Adrella Adams and this is my husband, Dathan."

When the name registered, her eyes lit with gratitude. "Oh, you be the one who stitched my Henry back together, the one who saved his life!" She grabbed Adrella's hand. "Your husband, he be an angel of God," she said fervently."

Adrella wasn't sure just how much of an angel he was, but she agreed that his gift came from God. She didn't think another man on this earth could have done the job that he did.

Dathan shifted uncomfortably and Adrella hid a smile.

He was always ill at ease under other people's praise. He pulled out the pouch that contained the funds collected by the other men and held it out to her.

"Mrs. Pierson, the men Henry works with took up a collection. They wanted you to have it."

Adrella didn't miss the fact that Dathan left out mentioning that he had added a large chunk of money as well.

When Dathan handed Mrs. Pierson the money, she burst into tears. Dathan passed her his handkerchief and she hastily wiped her eyes.

"Will you thank them for me, please?"

He nodded, his face that was so often devoid of emotion now drawn with the feelings he was trying to suppress.

"I will, you can be sure of it."

They spent a few more minutes with Henry and his mother and then took their leave. Dathan was quiet as they walked down the hall.

Before they left the ward a doctor in a white coat approached them.

"Dr. Adams?"

Dathan opened his mouth to object, but Adrella interceded.

"Yes, this is Dr. Adams. And you are?"

The man beamed at them both, though his look of admiration was for Dathan alone. "I'm Dr. Jared," he said, reaching his hand out to Dathan. "I just wanted to compliment you on the fine job of surgery you did on young Henry Pierson. I've never seen anything like it."

Dr. Jared was young, his face haggard with lack of sleep, yet his eyes were full of excitement.

Dathan slowly reached out to take the man's hand. "How is he doing?"

"He's doing as well as can be expected under the circumstances. So far there's been no fever, but then you probably noticed that already. We've decided to keep him chloroformed for a time so that his body has time to focus on healing. If you would like, I'd be happy to show you around."

Adrella had to hide a grin behind a cough. Young Dr. Jared was treating Dathan as though he had just descended from Mount Olympus.

"Another time, perhaps," Dathan answered smoothly. "I'm sure you are quite busy."

"Sure. Sure. Anytime. We could sure use a man like you," Dr. Jared continued. "Every hospital in the vicinity is full to overflowing with people hit by the hurricane. There are far more than we can manage."

Dathan stiffened. Adrella could see the pain from the resurfacing memories in his stormy gray eyes. She had seen that same look when he was faced with the enormous responsibility of saving Henry's life.

"Thank you for the compliment," Dathan said flatly. "If you'll excuse us, we have to catch a train."

Crestfallen, the young man hastily stepped back. "Of course. Forgive me."

Dathan almost pulled Adrella out of the building. Everywhere they looked, people were huddled waiting for a turn to see a doctor. Dathan's lips pressed into a grim line.

Adrella's heart went out to them. So much suffering. So many eyes filled with despair. She laid a hand on her husband's arm. "They could use you, Dathan."

"I have a light to attend to," he reminded her.

"Oh, my goodness, I almost forgot." In truth, when faced with such adversity, she hadn't given the lighthouse a second thought. She noticed the sun already beginning its afternoon descent. "Are we going to make it in time?" she asked anxiously.

He sighed heavily. "Probably not. We had to come farther inland than what I expected and with all the delays, we will never make it back to Apalach tonight."

Her eyes widened in alarm. "What are you going to do?"

"I'm going to see if I can find us a hotel for tonight. We'll have to stay the night and leave early in the morning."

Adrella was appalled. "But what about the light! It has to be lit, Dathan. There could be ships out there. More than likely there are! They could wreck!"

He placed a hand gently over her mouth to stem the rising tide of her fear-laced words.

"It's all right, Drell. I already planned for such an emergency." He moved his hand from her mouth and allowed it to settle on her shoulder reassuringly. "I showed Keith what to do in case we didn't make it back tonight."

Adrella blew out a breath of relief. "Oh. Did you know this would happen?"

He shook his head, placing both hands in the pockets of his pants. "I didn't know it, but I wasn't taking any chances. The hurricane did a lot of damage throughout these parts, so I had a feeling there would be problems even farther inland. It's what took our supplies so long to arrive."

She glanced around helplessly. "Where can we go? Don't you think all the hotels will be full?"

Taking her by the arm, he began walking back the way they had come. "Let's find out."

Dathan finally found them a room not far from the hospital. The cost was exorbitant, but that was the least of his concerns. He handed over the money without a qualm, giving the hotel clerk a look that let him know what he thought of the hotel's use of people's misfortune to make a dollar. The man had the grace to blush.

Adrella frowned. "We could have tried somewhere else."

He spoke slowly as if to let his words fall with effect. "Adrella, would you please stop worrying about money? You need to trust me on this."

She didn't answer, her straight shoulders letting him know just exactly how she felt. He smiled slightly, shaking his head at her stubbornness.

"Come on. Let's find our room."

The room was spacious and elegant. Adrella's mouth dropped open in surprise. He was watching her carefully.

"Do you like it?"

"Like it?" she squeaked. "Who wouldn't like it?"

His eyes met hers and held. "If you like it, then it was worth the price," he told her softly. "Get used to it, Adrella. I intend to spoil you like you've never been spoiled before."

Her face filled with soft color and he thought again how lovely she looked. The new dresses helped, but only in as much as they lifted her confidence. Adrella's beauty, he had already learned, came from within.

He pulled a roll of bills from his pocket and handed them to her. "I want you to go and have some fun."

She didn't reach for the money. "Me? What about you?"

"I thought I would go back and give a hand at the hospital."

His comment spoken in such a light way caught her off guard. She stared at him in stunned amazement, and no wonder. He was a bit amazed at himself. There was a part of him deep inside that had never felt right leaving the profession he had chosen. He had struggled with it over the years until he had finally wrangled it into submission. Now here he was about to do the very thing he swore he would never do again. Was he ready for it? He wasn't sure, but he knew he needed to try.

He knew that he had the power to help so many of those people who had huddled near the hospital. He might be a bit rusty, but young Henry had shown him that he hadn't lost the touch.

He was unprepared for the tears in Adrella's eyes. He racked his brain trying to figure out what he could have done to cause her pain.

"I'm so glad, Dathan," she whispered, tears lacing her voice. "I have been praying for you, that you would remember your calling."

He slid a forefinger along her cheek, watching the expressions on her face. Taking her hand, he placed the roll of bills in it, closing her fingers around it.

"Go have some fun," he told her huskily. "I don't know how long I will be. If I don't make it back in time for supper, you can either eat in the dining room or have it served to you here."

She nodded and he placed a quick kiss on her lips. Her startled look made him grin. Whistling, he left her staring after him.

Adrella awoke to sunlight streaming into the room. She sat up sleepily, noting the empty bed beside her. So Dathan hadn't made it back last night after all. Had that been deliberate? She had waited until long past midnight before she'd finally fallen asleep.

She heard the key in the lock and quickly pulled the covers up around her neck. She had used some of the money Dathan had given her to purchase some nightwear, not wanting to wrinkle her dress by sleeping in it. The nightgown was an impulse buy, more lovely than anything she had ever seen in Apalach and she hadn't been able to resist it. Now she regretted her hasty decision.

He looked tired when he came in.

"Have you been up all night?" she asked him, worried when she saw the dark circles under his eyes.

He nodded, going to the basin in the room, pouring some water from the pitcher and briskly rubbing his face with it. "I take it you haven't had breakfast yet?"

She shook her head, embarrassed to be caught sleeping so late.

"If you hurry and get dressed, we'll have time to eat before we head back to Apalach."

He seemed to note her huddling under the covers. One eyebrow winged upward, a wry smile tilting his lips. "I'll meet you in the dining room," he told her in amusement.

"How is Henry?"

He stopped with his hand on the doorknob. "Still alive." He glanced back at her. "I'll tell you more over breakfast. We have to hurry to make the morning train."

He left the room and Adrella scrambled to get ready.

The train whistle sounded, steam whooshing around the platform as they got ready to depart.

Dathan helped Adrella aboard with one hand while hanging on to her bags with the other. He had taken one look at all the things she had bought and grinned.

"It looks like you had fun."

She smiled back. "I did. I bought something for each one of the men."

He frowned. "I meant that money for you."

She shrugged. "I know, but I wanted to do something for the men. They were so good to give up so much of their pay for Henry."

He shook his head, the smile on his lips reaching all the way to his eyes. "Leave it to you. Did you buy anything for yourself?"

The color rushed into her face and his eyebrows flew

upward. Before she could answer, she was thankfully halted by the conductor's cry.

"All aboard."

They settled into their seats as the train began inching its way forward. Dathan stowed the packages on the seats across from them and sat down beside Adrella. She had just opened her mouth to say something when Dathan interrupted her.

"Adrella, there's something I need to say to you."

The clipped sound of his voice sent Adrella's heart plummeting to her toes. Uncertain of what was coming, she nodded her head, her wary look resting on Dathan's inscrutable face.

His eyes met hers, dark and intense. "Adrella, I'm in love with you."

Of all the things she had expected, that was certainly not it. She opened and closed her mouth several times.

"Well, of all the... You can't..." She glared at him, nonplussed. "What a thing to tell a girl in the middle of a crowded train!"

Lips twitching, eyes sparkling merrily, Dathan settled back against the seat, his long legs stretched out and crossed at the ankles, his arms crossed over his chest.

"I thought it might be safer."

Bristling, Adrella retaliated. "Safer? Safer for whom? Of all the..."

Dathan moved quickly, bringing his face close to hers. "Did you know that you're beautiful when you're angry?"

Adrella felt the starch leave her as quickly as it had surfaced. She searched his eyes for the truth, and found it.

"Well then, I'll just have to make certain sure that I stay angry, won't I?"

He grinned, wrapping one large hand behind her neck. "And I'll just have to make for certain sure that you're not."

When his eyes fastened on her lips, Adrella curled her toes into her shoes.

"Dathan, don't you dare!"

"I never have been able to resist a dare," he told her softly. Pulling her close, Adrella resisted only slightly. She had been longing for his kisses for some time now and they had been few and far between.

The intensity of the kiss left her breathless. There was a promise of more to come in Dathan's dark gray eyes.

"How long have you known?" Adrella asked him breathlessly, her eyes going to his lips still so close to hers.

"I don't know. I think I figured it out about the same time that I figured out that God had a plan for my life, and I let Him down."

Surprised, Adrella lifted her eyes to his. "You mean…?"

Dathan pulled her into the crook of his arm, settling back against the corner of the seat. She nestled her back against his chest.

"Yes, Adrella. I've decided to go back to being a doctor."

Turning her head upward where she could see his face, she said quietly, "You never really stopped, Dathan. Da, me, Henry, you've been there for all of us."

His voice was seductively low when he answered her. "And you, Drell? Will you be happy leaving the island?"

She turned full into his arms. "Whither thou goest, I will go. I love you, too, Dathan."

He traced a finger gently across her lips. "And your God will be my God."

Adrella willed the train to hurry, longing for Dathan to fulfill the promise she could see in his eyes. Not able to resist, she lifted herself up and gave him a quick kiss on the lips. Their eyes met once again, and they were oblivious of the stares of those around them, some outraged, others envious.

Something Adrella's father had said came back to her now.

"One day, Drell, you will wake up and find the place God made for you in this world, and you'll say, 'That's good.'"

Snuggling into Dathan's arms, she couldn't help but smile. Her place was with Dathan. *That's good,* she thought to herself. *That's so very good!*

Epilogue

Adrella carefully packed her father's green mug, placing it in the crate of dishes she was filling. She glanced around the small kitchen and a feeling of nostalgia overcame her.

For the past year this had been her home. Her home with Dathan.

The first day they had moved into their new house was indelibly etched into Adrella's memory. Dathan had carried her over the threshold to the laughing taunts of the men who had helped build it, those men who had seemed more like family than just workers. Even now, almost a year later, she missed that camaraderie. Most of them still kept in contact with her and Dathan.

She and Dathan had taken the new building and made it into more than a dwelling. This was the place where she and Dathan had become one.

Now that Dathan's contract with the Lighthouse Board was fulfilled, he had decided to go back to his home in

New York and become a doctor once again. He had relinquished the past and begun to look forward to a future. Without conceit, he had agreed that he did, indeed, have a gift, and he knew where that gift had come from.

They had talked it over for some time and, although Adrella would miss Apalachicola, it was really nothing without her father. She had meant it when she'd told Dathan that wherever he was, was home.

She went to the kitchen door and stared out for some time at the shimmering waters of the gulf, her thoughts wandering through time. Her father's body had never been found, but then, neither had some of the people in the vicinity.

"I miss you, Da," she whispered.

Her grief had faded, but not the memories. If she closed her eyes, she could still see her father's laughing green eyes, the lopsided grin that was so endearing.

Often when the wind soughed through the trees she could almost imagine hearing her father's voice. It was almost as clear to her as the voice of her other Father which she heard within herself. She knew without a doubt that they were both happy for her. She could feel it in the warm love that swelled through her whenever she thought of either one of them. The sense that things were right, as they were destined to be.

Her Da had somehow known that she and Dathan were meant to be together, but it took her Father in heaven to make it happen. It made her smile to think of her father standing in the presence of the Almighty, both of them happy with the way things had turned out.

She had been married to Dathan for a year, and yet she still thrilled at the thought that he loved her. In her wildest imaginings she could never had foreseen such happiness as she felt at this moment.

She went back to packing the few items they would be taking with them and the happiness dwindled at the shiver of anxiety that coursed through her. She would be meeting Dathan's family soon. What would they think of her? If they were expecting a lovely debutante, they were going to be sorely disappointed. It still worried her that she might do something to embarrass her husband.

Something bumping against her leg brought her thoughts back to the moment at hand. Glancing down, she smiled.

"Hello, Grace."

Reaching down, she lifted the cat into her arms, cuddling her close. Rubbing her nose against Grace's soft fur, Adrella had to smile at the resulting purr. She held the cat up, looking into her eyes. The black patch surrounding her one eye gave her the appearance of a pirate. It always made Adrella smile.

"Are you ready for your new home?" she asked.

A soft meow was the only answer she received.

"At least I'll have you, won't I?"

Strong arms wrapped around her from behind, startling her. She gave a slight yelp.

"You have me, too. Don't I count?"

Adrella smiled, turning into the circle of his arms. Grace gave a slight meow of protest at being so confined.

Dathan released Adrella and, taking the cat from her arms, put her out the back door.

"If you don't mind," he told the cat, "this is a personal conversation."

Adrella chuckled at his teasing statement, but when he turned back to her, his face was solemn. He wrapped her closely in his arms again, his eyes studying her carefully. Adrella hated it when he did that because it was as though he truly could read her mind. Not that she wanted to keep anything from him, but at times it was decidedly uncomfortable.

"Drell, my parents will love you. They would love you anyway just because I do, but no one could help but love you just for you."

From past experience she rather doubted that. Still, her husband was tense enough at this meeting without having to worry about her as well. Wrinkling her nose, she sighed. "I'm just being silly, I suppose."

He continued to search her features and Adrella sighed again more loudly.

"Would you please stop doing that!" she said.

One corner of his mouth tilted up. "Doing what? Staring at my beautiful wife?"

Adrella gave him an eloquent look at this obvious falsehood, but her cheeks warmed nonetheless at his compliment. "You know exactly what I mean."

He laughed outright at that. Capturing her face between his palms he proceeded to give her a kiss that would have erased anything from her mind, much less niggling doubts about her future.

He smiled, staring hard into her eyes. "I love you, Drell. You know that, don't you?"

She returned his smile, her heart melting at the love she saw shining in his eyes. "I know. I love you, too."

A sound at the back door caught Dathan's attention.

"Mr. Adams, I'm ready for that tour."

Dathan released Adrella, nodding his head at the replacement keeper. "I'll be right with you." He touched a finger to Adrella's nose. "I'll leave you to your packing."

Adrella watched him leave, her heart overflowing with emotion.

"You have a lovely wife."

Dathan smiled at the new keeper. "Thanks, Ed. I think so."

It was true. Adrella grew more beautiful to him every day. Whenever he told her so, she always told him that if it was true, it was only because of his love. That made perfect sense to him, since his love for her grew more every day as well. At times he thought his heart would burst from his chest with the strength of his feelings.

For so many years he had thought he was happy to be alone. Now he didn't envy this man who was replacing him. There would be no Mangus Murphy to befriend him, to bring him supplies, although it was possible that there was an Adrella waiting in the wings. He paused. No, that wasn't possible, either, because there was only one Adrella and she belonged to him.

He glanced at the other man. "Are you married, Ed?"

Ed shook his head. "Never had the time."

Dathan wondered what had taken so much of the man's time but didn't think it his place to ask. In the end, he didn't need to.

"I worked on a sailing ship before the war. I remember the safe feeling whenever we got close to harbor and saw the lights from the lighthouses wherever we went. I decided that I wanted to give that same feeling to others. I was told how hard it was to get people to man the lights."

Dathan silently agreed. They drew up in front of the newly built oil house. "The loneliness gets to most people."

He opened the door and they went inside. After explaining the layout and the times of refueling from the Lighthouse Board, they headed over to the light tower.

Ed stopped for a moment and stared out over the gulf. The waves were calm today. Gulls circled overhead in a never-ending search for sustenance.

"It sure looks peaceful," he remarked.

Remembering last year's hurricane and subsequent storms, Dathan had to smile.

"Looks can be deceiving."

Hadn't he learned that even from his own wife? What he had at one time considered plain and unappealing had turned out to hide a true treasure. The Bible spoke of God looking for what was on the inside of a man. What others saw as worthless, God saw differently. If only people would do the same. He had certainly learned his lesson well. First Adrella, then Henry.

As they toured the light, Dathan's mind went back to that fateful day of the worst hurricane this part of the country had ever seen. Even now he could see Adrella sitting on that iron step working her fingers through her hair. He had been happy here. He was going to miss it.

"I understand there's a problem with the lens," Ed stated, interrupting Dathan's introspection. He reluctantly pulled himself back to the present.

"Yes, it was damaged in the war."

A darkness settled over the other man's features. "A lot of things were damaged in the war."

It was a statement that needed no qualifying. Hoping to turn his thinking from obviously morose thoughts, Dathan placed a hand on the other man's shoulder.

"My wife made lunch. We'd like it if you would share it with us."

In an instant Ed's face cleared. "I'd like that."

They finished the tour and returned to the cottage.

Adrella stood with Dathan on the pier watching, with her heart in her throat, the boat being rowed to shore from the ship sitting placidly farther out in the gulf. She was about to meet her father-in-law for the first time.

Dathan's father had come in his own private clipper ship to pick them up and bring them back to New York. The ship was impressive in size, the long masts rising high against the blue of the afternoon sky, the sails bound tightly to the masts awaiting the word to set sail again. She was only now beginning to understand the true extent of the wealth she had by marriage inherited.

As if sensing her trepidation, Dathan took her hand and gently squeezed it. She glanced up at him, her nerves settling somewhat at the love she saw shining from his eyes.

The rowboat neared shore and it was clear which man was Dathan's father among its seven occupants. He sat in the center of the boat, his dress and manner so obviously above those who were manning the oars. The shadow of his hat hid most of his face from view but he was, nonetheless, a commanding presence. Adrella could picture him stepping from the boat into a boardroom of supplicants.

When the boat reached the dock, Dathan took the mooring line and tied it to the pier.

Dathan's father looked up from the place where he sat and Adrella could see where Dathan's good looks had come from. This would be what Dathan would look like in another twenty years. Eyes the same color of gray as her husband's studied her curiously before turning to Dathan.

"Hello, Father." Dathan reached out a hand to help his father onto the dock.

He took the proffered hand. "Dathan."

They studied each other several seconds before Mr. Adams turned to her.

"So this is my daughter." He acknowledged her presence in one all-encompassing glance. Although she might be lacking in beauty, there could be no faulting the beautiful gown she wore. Having overcome her aversion to green, she knew the dress set off her flaming hair and emerald-green eyes in a way no other could. It had been Dathan's choice, and it was her favorite.

"It's good to finally meet you," Mr. Adams told her.

Adrella was surprised that there was no censure in the look her gave her. Instead his eyes held only friendly interest.

He took her hand, lifted it to his lips and placed a soft kiss there. The courteous gesture sent the color to her cheeks and Dathan's brows flying to his hairline.

He held on to her hand as he turned to his son. "Your mother wanted to come, but she has been ill. I left her on the ship." He smiled at Adrella. "She's impatient to meet you."

This kind of greeting was not at all what Adrella had expected. From everything Dathan had told her, she had expected to be treated to cool disdain, not this warm cordiality. She beamed a smile at her father-in-law. "As I am, her."

He finally released her hand and turned to his son. "It's good to see you, son."

Adrella could see the tension ease from Dathan's shoulders. "And you, Dad."

Mr. Adams glanced at the suitcases on the dock, along with the few crates. His eyebrows lifted at the cat carrier, but he said nothing about it.

"Is this all you have?" he questioned in surprise.

Dathan nodded. "We decided to leave most of our things for the new lighthouse keeper."

Adrella couldn't quite read the expression on Mr. Adams's face. He was very much like his son in that respect.

"Well then. Let's get you loaded up and the men can come back for your things."

He helped Adrella into the rowboat, settling himself

onto the seat beside her. Dathan climbed into the boat and seated himself across from them, throwing Adrella a reassuring smile.

Dathan glanced at his father. "What's wrong with Mother?"

"Nothing, now. But she had a bad case of influenza."

There was something in the way he delivered the words that said there was more to the story than that. Infinitely more. Dathan must have sensed it, too.

Leaning forward, his face creased with concern, Dathan asked, "How bad?"

Mr. Adams focused his look on his hands twisting in his lap. "She almost died, Dathan."

His soft voice sent goose bumps racing along Adrella's arms. She caught her breath at the same time Dathan did.

"And you never told me?" Dathan asked angrily.

"She asked me not to."

The hurt look that flashed across Dathan's face brought a lump to Adrella's throat.

Mr. Adams looked up at his son, his lips set in a grim line. "And it's not for the reasons you are thinking."

Before he could comment, they reached the ship and one of the sailors stood and threw the bowline to a man waiting on deck. Two sailors began lowering a wooden seat by a pulley system. Adrella swallowed hard, knowing it was to bring her onto the ship so that she wouldn't have to climb the rope ladder that the men used. Dathan carefully helped her onto it, his warm hands closing reassuringly over hers where they tightly clenched the rope.

His eyes met hers encouragingly. "You'll be fine."

She gave him a lame smile, nodding.

Dathan looked up. "Bring her aboard," he shouted and the chair began its jerking ascent.

* * *

Dathan watched with his heart in his mouth as Adrella was lifted aboard his father's ship. He stood tense, ready to intervene in case anything happened. He didn't release his breath until she was pulled over the side and gave him a little wave from the deck. He was thankful that she hadn't seen Grace's cat carrier being thrown to a sailor aboard the clipper.

His father had already ascended the rope ladder and Dathan quickly scaled it behind him.

Adrella met him at the top, her face only now beginning to regain some color. Placing his hands on her shoulders, he studied her carefully.

"Are you all right?"

"Fine. It was rather fun, really."

Dathan smiled. His indomitable Adrella. He took her hand when his father motioned them to follow him below.

Mr. Adams knocked softly on the door to his quarters before opening it. He stepped back to allow them passage into the room.

Sunlight from several portholes brightened the room, exposing its contents. Lushly appointed with the finest furniture money could buy, this was the life he remembered so well.

His mother was sitting up in bed, a pale shadow of the woman he remembered. She was thin to the point of emaciation, her bed jacket doing nothing to hide the bones protruding from her shoulders. He had only seen such emaciation during the war. It made plain to him just how ill his mother had been. He would never have forgiven himself if she had died with the breach between them still unresolved. He swallowed hard, trying to dislodge the knot that had formed in his throat.

"Mother." He quickly crossed to the bed and knelt at

her side. He took her thin hand into his own and brought it to his lips. "Why didn't you tell me?"

"I didn't want your bride to see me like I was. I'm much better now."

If this was better, he could only imagine what her illness had done to her.

"How long have you been ill?"

"Several weeks," his father answered for her, the timbre of his voice telling Dathan more than anything just how close his mother had come to leaving this earth.

"We received your letter just before I became ill," she explained. "We knew that you would have much to do to get ready to come home. We thought it best."

She looked past his shoulder. "But enough of that. Introduce me to your lovely bride."

Adrella came forward and took Dathan's outstretched hand. He could feel her trembling, yet her face held a genuine smile.

"Adrella, this is my mother. Mother, this is the love of my life."

"Adrella. What an unusual name."

Dathan was surprised at the genuine warmth that filled his mother's pale face. She reached forward and took Adrella's other hand.

"My dear, I am so pleased to meet you. Dathan has spoken of you so much in his letters that I feel like I know you." She patted the side of the bed. "Won't you sit down and let us get to know you?"

This meeting hadn't gone anything like what Dathan had been expecting. He stared from one parent to the other, perplexed. Something had changed. There was a gentleness about them both that hadn't been there before.

They all spent a few minutes chatting and then Dathan's father cleared his throat.

"Dathan, we want to apologize to you."

A worried frown creased Dathan's forehead. What on earth was going on here? He had never heard his father apologize to anyone in his life.

His father continued. "We forced you to decide between your faith and us. That was wrong of us."

His father moved to the other side of the bed and took the hand Dathan's mother held out to him. "We have a story to tell you. Please be patient and allow us to finish it before you say anything," he said.

Dathan nodded his assent, feeling as though the world had just turned topsy-turvy.

"Your mother had influenza so bad that her life hung by a thread for many days." He swallowed hard and Dathan knew it was difficult for him to continue. He had never doubted the love his parents had for each other, although he had doubted their love for him.

"The nurse who tended her was a godly woman. Irish, as a matter of fact." His father smiled at Adrella and Dathan saw the color rush to her face.

"She spent a lot of time reading to your mother, mainly from the Bible. I could see that the words brought your mother comfort, and then, they began to bring me comfort as well." He sighed heavily. "I began to pray. I have never prayed for anything so hard in my life, not even for your and your brother's safety. In my arrogance I didn't think I needed to."

His mother squeezed his father's hand and they looked at each other the way Dathan and Adrella looked at each other. It was a merging of the hearts.

"Anyway," he continued, "the Lord showed us that we were not as self-sufficient as we thought we were."

Adrella's voice chimed in softly. "You found the Lord."

His father glanced at her. "That, and a whole lot more."

That would explain the difference that Dathan had sensed. The gentleness that had always been missing from their home was now clear to see. What would his life had been like if their home had always had this kind of peace? He could only imagine. But then he might not have ever met Adrella. That thought brought him up short. He only now realized that he would not give up a single minute of the life he had lived if it meant he would not have her.

"Can you forgive us?" his mother asked.

The feelings he had struggled with all his life melted away under the questioning gazes of both of his parents. Reaching down, he wrapped his mother in a gentle hug, fearful that he might harm her.

"I love you," he told them, including both of them in his look.

He caught Adrella's liquid look as he struggled to hold back his own tears. It was time for the healing to begin for all of them.

Adrella watched the shores of Cape St. George Island receding in the distance.

Dathan wrapped her in his arms and they silently watched that part of their life recede forever.

"I'm going to miss it," he told her softly.

Adrella swallowed hard. As would she. Apalachicola was the only life she could remember.

"Are you sorry, Drell? Should we have stayed?"

Adrella turned fully in his arms so that she could look him in the eye. It had never occurred to her that he might be feeling uncertain as well.

"Whither thou goest." Laying a palm against his cheek, she answered back, "As long as we are together, Dathan, anywhere is home."

"I feel the same way about you," he told her quietly.

She stood silently taking in all that had transpired in the past several hours. The genuine warmth of his parents had banished the last traces of her fears. They had made her feel like a part of their family. It was amazing how the Lord had worked in their lives to show them His love, and to bring reconciliation.

"I like your parents," she stated quietly.

He smiled, tightening his hold. "I think the feeling is mutual." His look became thoughtful. "I never gave up praying for them, hoping they would come to see what the Lord truly means in a person's life."

"'For the eyes of the Lord are over the righteous, and his ears are open unto their prayers,'" she quoted. "And you are a righteous man, my love," she finished huskily.

His kiss expressed more than words ever could have. They turned back to watch the setting of the sun, the glorious shades of red and orange bursting over the water. As the band of twilight deepened, a bright beam of light from Cape St. George Light shot out across the darkening sea.

* * * * *

REQUEST YOUR FREE BOOKS!

2 FREE CHRISTIAN NOVELS
PLUS 2
FREE
MYSTERY GIFTS

HEARTSONG
PRESENTS

YES! Please send me 2 Free Heartsong Presents novels and my 2 FREE mystery gifts (gifts are worth about $10). After receiving them, if I don't wish to receive any more books I can return the shipping statement marked "cancel." If I don't cancel, I will receive 4 brand-new novels every month and be billed just $4.24 per book. That's a savings of 20% off the cover price. It's quite a bargain! Shipping and handling is just 50¢ per book in the U.S.* I understand that accepting the 2 free books and gifts places me under no obligation to buy anything. I can always return a shipment and cancel at any time. Even if I never buy another book, the two free books and gifts are mine to keep forever.

159 HDN FVYK

Name	(PLEASE PRINT)

Address	Apt. #

City	State	Zip

Signature (if under 18, a parent or guardian must sign)

Mail to the Harlequin® Reader Service:
IN U.S.A.: P.O. Box 1867, Buffalo, NY 14240-1867

* Terms and prices subject to change without notice. Prices do not include applicable taxes. Sales tax applicable in N.Y. This offer is limited to one order per household. Not valid for current subscribers to Heartsong Presents books. All orders subject to credit approval. Credit or debit balances in a customer's account(s) may be offset by any other outstanding balance owed by or to the customer. Please allow 4 to 6 weeks for delivery. Offer available while quantities last. Offer valid only in the U.S.

Your Privacy—The Harlequin® Reader Service is committed to protecting your privacy. Our Privacy Policy is available online at www.ReaderService.com or upon request from the Harlequin Reader Service.
We make a portion of our mailing list available to reputable third parties that offer products we believe may interest you. If you prefer that we not exchange your name with third parties, or if you wish to clarify or modify your communication preferences, please visit us at www.ReaderService.com/consumerschoice or write to us at Harlequin Reader Service Preference Service, P.O. Box 9062, Buffalo, NY 14269. Include your complete name and address.

HSPDIR13

REQUEST YOUR FREE BOOKS!

2 FREE INSPIRATIONAL NOVELS
PLUS 2
FREE
MYSTERY GIFTS

Love Inspired
HISTORICAL
INSPIRATIONAL HISTORICAL ROMANCE

YES! Please send me 2 FREE Love Inspired® Historical novels and my 2 FREE mystery gifts (gifts are worth about $10). After receiving them, if I don't wish to receive any more books, I can return the shipping statement marked "cancel." If I don't cancel, I will receive 4 brand-new novels every month and be billed just $4.49 per book in the U.S. or $4.99 per book in Canada. That's a savings of at least 22% off the cover price. It's quite a bargain! Shipping and handling is just 50¢ per book in the U.S. and 75¢ per book in Canada.* I understand that accepting the 2 free books and gifts places me under no obligation to buy anything. I can always return a shipment and cancel at any time. Even if I never buy another book, the two free books and gifts are mine to keep forever.

102/302 IDN FV2V

Name	(PLEASE PRINT)	
Address		Apt. #
City	State/Prov.	Zip/Postal Code

Signature (if under 18, a parent or guardian must sign)

Mail to the Harlequin® Reader Service:
IN U.S.A.: P.O. Box 1867, Buffalo, NY 14240-1867
IN CANADA: P.O. Box 609, Fort Erie, Ontario L2A 5X3

Want to try two free books from another series?
Call 1-800-873-8635 or visit www.ReaderService.com.

* Terms and prices subject to change without notice. Prices do not include applicable taxes. Sales tax applicable in N.Y. Canadian residents will be charged applicable taxes. Offer not valid in Quebec. This offer is limited to one order per household. Not valid for current subscribers to Love Inspired Historical books. All orders subject to credit approval. Credit or debit balances in a customer's account(s) may be offset by any other outstanding balance owed by or to the customer. Please allow 4 to 6 weeks for delivery. Offer available while quantities last.

Your Privacy—The Harlequin® Reader Service is committed to protecting your privacy. Our Privacy Policy is available online at www.ReaderService.com or upon request from the Harlequin Reader Service.

We make a portion of our mailing list available to reputable third parties that offer products we believe may interest you. If you prefer that we not exchange your name with third parties, or if you wish to clarify or modify your communication preferences, please visit us at www.ReaderService.com/consumerschoice or write to us at Harlequin Reader Service Preference Service, P.O. Box 9062, Buffalo, NY 14269. Include your complete name and address.

LIHDIR13

HEARTSONG
PRESENTS

Look out for 4 new
Heartsong Presents books next month!

**Every month 4 inspiring faith-filled
romances will be available in stores.**

These contemporary and historical Christian
romances emphasize God's role in every
relationship and reinforce the importance of
faith, hope and love.

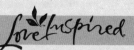
Jolie followed Morgan outside. There was a large gnarled oak tree still bent over as it had been all those years ago. She didn't stop until she reached it, turning his way only after they were beneath the wide expanse of limbs.

Morgan crossed his arms and studied the tree. "I remember having to climb up this tree and talk you down after you scrambled up to the top and froze."

She hadn't expected him to bring up old memories—it caught her a little off guard. "I remember how mad you were at having to rescue the silly little new girl."

A hint of a smile teased his lips, fraying Jolie's nerves at the edges. It had been a long time since she'd seen that smile.

"I got used to it, though," he said, his voice warming.

Electricity hummed between them as they stared at each other. Jolie sucked in a wobbly breath. Then the hardness in Morgan's tone matched the accusation in his eyes.

"What are you doing here, Jolie? Why aren't you taming rapids in some far-off place?"

"I…I'm—" She stumbled over her words. "I'm taking a leave from competition for a little while. I had a bad run in Virginia." She couldn't bring herself to say that she'd almost died. "Your dad offered me this teaching opportunity."

"I heard about the accident and I'm real sorry about that, Jolie," Morgan said. "But why come here after all this time?"

"This is my *home.*"

Jolie saw anger in Morgan's eyes. Well, he had a right to it, and more than a right to point it straight at her.

But she'd thought she'd prepared for it.

She was wrong.

"Morgan," Jolie said, almost as a whisper. "I'd hoped we could forget the past and move forward."

Heart pounding, she reached across the space between them and placed her hand on his arm. It was just a touch, but the feeling of connecting with Morgan McDermott again after so much time rocked her straight to her core, and suddenly she wasn't so sure coming home had been the right thing to do after all.

Will Morgan ever allow Jolie back into
his life—and his heart?

Pick up HER UNFORGETTABLE COWBOY
from Love Inspired Books.

LIEXP0413RR

Love Inspired

Will You Marry Me?

Bold widow Johanna Yoder stuns Roland Byler when she asks him to be her husband. To Johanna, it seems very sensible that they marry. She has two children, he has a son. Why shouldn't their families become one? But the widower has never forgotten his long-ago love for her; it was his foolish mistake that split them apart. This could be a fresh start for both of them—until she reveals she wants a marriage of convenience only. It's up to Roland to woo the stubborn Johanna and convince her to accept him as her groom in her home and in her heart.

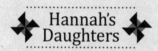

Hannah's Daughters

Johanna's Bridegroom

by

Emma Miller

Available May 2013

www.LoveInspiredBooks.com

LI8781

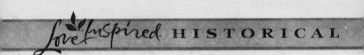

Love Inspired HISTORICAL

In the fan-favorite miniseries
Cowboys of Eden Valley

LINDA FORD

presents

The Cowboy's Convenient Proposal

Second Chance Ranch

She is a woman in need of protection. But trust is the one thing feisty Grace "Red" Henderson is sure she'll never give any man again—not even the cowboy who rescued her. Still, Ward Walker longs to protect the wary beauty and her little sister—in all the ways he couldn't safeguard his own family.

Red desperately wants to put her tarnished past behind her. Little by little, Ward is persuading her to take a chance on Eden Valley, and on him. Yet turning his practical proposal into a real marriage means a leap of faith for both…toward a future filled with the promise of love.

COWBOYS
OF
Eden Valley

Available May 2013

www.LoveInspiredBooks.com